Jumping Over the Moon

A novel by

E Dee Monnen

Robert D. Reed Publishers
P.O. Box 1992
Bandon, OR 97411
Phone: 541-347-9882; Fax: -9883
E-mail: 4bobreed@msn.com
Website: www.rdrpublishers.com

Cover Art: The Lakota headdress featured on the cover is an illustration by Steve McAfee interpreted from an original photograph by Walter Larrimore © National Museum of the American Indian, Smithsonian Institution.
Cover Designer: Steve McAfee
Book Designer: Debby Gwaltney
Author Photo: Charles F. Monnen, Jr.

ISBN 13: 978-1-934759-59-2
ISBN 10: 1-934759-59-7

Library of Congress Control Number: 2011937946

Manufactured, Typeset, and Printed in the United States of America

In memory of

Sylvia M. (Bergen) Young

Sylvia M. Young passed on July 12, 2008,
at the age of 94.
She was also known as

"Masaska Win." Masa means Iron,
Ska white (silver) and Win woman.

She was loved by many.

Akewachinyakinkte

ACKNOWLEDGMENTS

I wish to thank my Lakota friends from South Dakota, Bill Gayton, Sylvia M. Bergen Young, and Wilma Fielder, also known as *Kimimila Win which means Butterfly Woman.* Their knowledge of the Lakota language and culture was invaluable to me.

Additional thanks go to William Haase, Rick Kollinger, and Rebecca Stefanski for answering all of my baseball questions both historical and technical.

Several sets of eyes were essential on this project, and all of my readers deserve my heartfelt thanks, Rebecca Stefanski, Wilma Fielder, Eric Monnen, Charles Monnen, Helen Monnen, Julie Christensen, Mary Waltenberger, Faye Quam Heimerl, Rick Kollinger, and my editor Amy Harke-Moore.

Finally, I must give special thanks to those who helped in other ways: Jeanne Robinson for assisting me on my first trip to South Dakota, and Susan Ross for helping me on my second trip; Chip Monnen for his photography; Andrea Berg for her artistic guidance; Betsy Grace for her never-ending stream of encouragement, and my husband Eric for all of his love and support.

I wish to thank Robert D. Reed Publishers, Bob and Cleone, for believing in my book.

I am indebted to all the above mentioned friends and family members for their contributions to this book.

Before the 1930s, Major League players were allowed to play for independent teams and leagues during the offseason, and Los Angeles was a favored winter venue. With concerns over injuries and a strong desire to protect their own interests, both the American and National League clubs later prohibited players from contracting with other teams.

The photo featured below represents one of the last baseball teams from the Indian Industrial School in Carlisle, Pennsylvania. When school administrators recognized their students' tremendous athletic abilities, they kept them from playing against professional farm teams, fearing they would be signed by Major League clubs and not complete their education.

Photo credit: The U.S. Army Military History Institution

~ CHAPTER ONE ~

Rural Los Angeles
1880s

I was promised a race, not a test of every nerve in my body.

When I left home, the fog was light, but during the race, all I could see were Thunder's bobbing ears and mane. Not comprehending how foolish I was, I rode at a breakneck speed, determined never to quit and betray victory by chickening out.

My friend Morton Cunningham had made all the arrangements.

"Hey, Phin," he said to me. "Jake Wooten's stable boy Tommy has a funeral to attend, so I volunteered to exercise Jake's thoroughbreds this Sunday. What do you think? Care to join me?"

Even at fifteen, I was skeptical. Mr. Wooten wouldn't trust Mort with his champion horses. But Mort's family was very prominent in the community, so I could hardly doubt him. Perhaps the arrangement was made by Mort's father.

"I don't know," I told him. "It sounds like work."

"Exercising horses isn't always work. I think it all depends on a person's definition of exercise. It could mean walk, trot, gallop, or even an all out run. And if it means run, we could make a race out of it!"

"Race?" Mort was so convincing, like a natural born salesman. "That would be fun," I told him, "but I'll be expected in church with my family. Not going would cross Father."

"They're champions, Phin. You'll never get a chance like this again. You've watched them by the fence. They're mighty fast animals."

I had to agree. This was a once in a lifetime opportunity, but I wasn't lucky like Mort. He often bragged about never getting caught, while I had a dismal record of avoiding the belt. The fear of Father usually motivated me to be on my best behavior; though skipping church for a chance to ride a great horse seemed like a worthy exception. So, I snuck out during the pastor's opening prayer.

As a warm-up, we rode about a mile down the Anaheim-Telegraph Road where Mort stopped and turned. "When I say *go*, we'll race back to Wooten's property—the leading edge of his lane will be the finish line."

I had partially turned my horse around when Mort yelled, "GO!"

I wasn't ready, but Thunder was. He blazed down the road, passing Mort and leaving him a reasonable distance behind.

With the wind in my face and the feel of brute strength beneath me, I thrived on this new level of speed. Thunder lived up to his name and was the finest horse I had ever ridden.

"Let's do it, Thunder!" We charged forward, confident our course would be free of all traffic during church, until we came upon a fellow who was about to cross the road. He was startled by the beating hooves and then two horses which suddenly emerged from the dense fog. His near brush with death caused him to loose his footing and fall backward into the ditch.

"Hey, you hooligans!" he yelled.

It was a short race, so I knew Wooten's lane wasn't much farther. And then, there it was, coming into view through a break in the fog. Mort began to close in on my right, but without any further encouragement, Thunder surged ahead. No doubt about it—my horse wanted the lead position. We won by two lengths.

I cupped my hands around my mouth and yelled, "I won—I'm the greatest rider in Los Angeles County!"

"You looked good back there," Mort replied, as we started a cool-down walk.

"Looked good? What do you mean? I was GREAT!" I shouted with unbounded enthusiasm. I expected Mort's usual verbal barbs, but instead, he sounded nervous and subdued—my first hint something was wrong.

We dismounted and walked the horses back to the barn, recapping the race along the way.

"Oh, come on, Mort. You were never in the lead. Admit it, I was sensational."

"Okay—you were, but you don't have to shout."

"What do you mean? Of course, I must." I cupped my hands again and was about to yell when Mort grabbed my arm.

"Hey, stop that! Not so loud. Sound travels farther in the fog, and one of Wooten's neighbors might hear you."

"So? Maybe I'll tell them, too."

"You can't. We rode without permission."

"Huh?" I pulled my horse to a stop—stunned by what I had just heard. "You mean we stole these horses!" My jaw tightened as I grimaced through my teeth to hold back what I really wanted to say.

"Shh! Or you'll really get us in trouble. I paid Tommy to keep his mouth shut, and I'm not paying off the entire southland."

I felt sick and full of anguish—betrayed by my best friend. My thrill of victory fizzled to thoughts of five to ten on a chain gang. I was angry for trusting Mort. All I could think about were the current laws for stealing horses and Father's displeasure and shame. What have I done? This was no longer a simple matter of skipping church. Overcome by fear and remorse, I expected to see Mr. Wooten and Father behind every shrub and at every turn. What should I do? Outrun the law? Leave my family forever? Why did I do this? I shouldn't face judgment when I didn't know.

Woo-OO'-hoo-hoo-hoo, I heard the mourning doves cooing in the distance. My impending demise certainly gave them something to mourn over. Sweat began to seep from every pore on my body, but rather than face the dire consequences of the law or the wrath of Father, my mind shifted with lingering feelings of nausea, dread, and agony.

Woo-OO'-hoo-hoo-hoo, again I heard the mourning doves, but this time, they cooed outside my bedroom balcony. Their version of reveille was followed indoors by a soft breeze and a light scent of eucalyptus. What happened long ago was far from any concern today. By some miracle, Mort and I managed to return and brush down both horses before Mr. Wooten arrived home, although over the years, I often wondered if he had noticed anything unusual that day.

I sat up in bed, filled my lungs with the fresh air, and exhaled a big sigh of relief. It was only natural that I should have the recurring nightmare—it was race day, and I was up for another challenge against Mort. With joyful enthusiasm, I mimicked the doves' sunrise melody, though sounding more like a lone coyote than a feathered friend.

Maggie rolled over and yanked the sheet over her head. "Phineas Gannon, you silly man." She giggled under the bedding. "Don't you think the music should be left to the professionals? The birds do a much better job." Her soft hand tickled my side.

"Ah, but this is my big day when I show Mort who's the better competitor." I pulled back the cover just enough to kiss my beautiful wife. Her soft lips were as sweet as the first time they met mine thirty years ago. I stroked her cheek with the back of my fingers, brushing back a small lock of hair. She had only a few wisps of gray in her auburn bob—probably caused by my competitions with Mort.

"I have a funny victory speech prepared. It's a doozey. Like to hear it?"

"No." She chuckled and returned a kiss. "I want to give you a fresh reaction tonight when you read it at your victory party."

She was always a good sport at these events. For this occasion, I pictured my dearest Maggie sitting by my side, gazing at me with great admiration, while I entertained our guests with delightful humor.

Mort and I were very successful entrepreneurs, so our competitions were never about the money. It was only our way of keeping score. Mort was the last to win, and he had been gloating ever since. I'd never admit it, but his constant bragging got on my nerves. That was why I wagered $200, the same amount I lagged behind, if only to stop him from wallowing in his pride. It was a high stake, but this time all the physical advantages were mine. Without question, I'd be declared the winner and at even money with Mort before nightfall—but that wasn't quite the way it turned out.

~ CHAPTER TWO ~

September 1928

Around four in the afternoon, my longtime friend Duke Maner stopped by our ranch. He was the one person who shared my child-like exuberance on competition days. It was our plan to ride together to the track, and because temperatures hovered around a hundred degrees, we decided to show up shortly before the start.

Duke was a little older than I, tall, and rather handsome—a retired baseball pitcher and local celebrity, who, over the years, was able to maintain his athletic appearance. Duke saw Mort and me as modern day gladiators, expressing our innermost desires to be the best at sport and never minding the strong smell of sweat in the arena. He understood the mysterious forces that propelled us toward victory, crediting the striving as much as the destination. But with my strong competitive nature came a spirit of compassion which tempered my masculine aggressions—influences encouraged in me by Mother. Perhaps if mankind could foster this gentler side, there may never be another Great War like what we had experienced in Europe a decade ago. Organized sport could then supplant deadly combat.

I parked my Cadillac in a nearby field where a couple hundred cars had already filled the wide expanse.

"At last," I told Duke, with a slight skip in my step as we headed toward the designated course. "I'm going to give Mort a real run for his money."

Duke laughed. "Phin, how many times have I heard you say that?"

I supposed he was right. Over the years Mort and I had waged several public competitions in balloon, sailboat, and motor bike racing—just to name a few. They were exhilarating duels we could well afford. It was only an unexpected consequence when we realized our outrageous competitions could be incorporated into marketing bonanzas for the benefit of our companies. When given adequate press coverage, they attracted record numbers of excited fans. For our latest crowd pleaser, we chose the modern race car.

Months earlier, Mort contacted a racing enthusiast from Santa Monica and offered him a tidy sum to lease two of his high-powered racers. We wanted the ones with the Miller engines which were powerful enough to fly airplanes. The owner agreed as long as he could provide the drivers. We cut cards for the choice of man. I won that round and chose the highly acclaimed Jimmy Green, which made me the odds on favorite to win.

The Miller cars were designed to race in a bowl arena, and it was our original plan to use the Motordome, a circular board track located on the west side of Los Angeles. But since the Motordome was too far away and too expensive to rent, we improvised by using a paved public road that dead-ended on the edge of an oil field. The total distance of our course was just under three miles. The first part was a mile and a half on a straight section of the road. From there, it continued uphill onto a dirt access road and circled around a lonely oil derrick that stood proudly atop a gentle knoll. And finally, it backtracked onto the same paved road toward the finish line.

Photographers from Los Angeles newspapers had come early to set up and were continually vying for position and adjusting their equipment, each professional hoping to snap the best picture of the winner roaring across the finish line. All in all, our choice of racecourse proved to be a great benefit. Unlike the steeply banked bowl arena, our open straightaway allowed unlimited numbers of curiosity seekers free and easy access to our event.

It was Duke's brilliant idea to use a public road outside Santa Fe Springs and tie the race to the hospital's carnival fundraiser being held on the adjacent field. He had convinced the local authorities to close the section of road for about an hour, suggesting our race could attract hundreds more people to the charitable event. The sheriff's department was especially cooperative once they realized it could help a worthy cause, and as usual, Duke's pull with dignitaries and politicians never ceased to amaze Mort and me.

"Step right up!" the pitchman shouted through his megaphone after removing a cigar stub from his mouth. "That's right, buy a refreshing soft drink, and get a free Silver Suds shaving mug. There's no finer lather on earth for your rough beard than Silver Suds," he continued his claims while perched on a lifeguard's platform shaded by a large umbrella.

Mort capitalized on every race by making sure endless supplies of free soap samplers were available as promotional items. All were custom shaped to fit inside his company's unique shaving mugs.

Using pitchmen whenever possible, we depended on successful food and beverage sales to help defray the cost of our competitions. Our best barkers were carnies from the Long Beach Pike. They knew exactly how to encourage concession sales—though I wished they wouldn't say Mort's products were used by Scandinavian kings and Mideast sultans.

"…And don't leave without two or three Gannon prime beef sandwiches," the pitchman continued. "It's the leanest and most delectable beef—desired worldwide but produced and sold only in Southern California."

Mort and I had agreed to stand on opposite sides of the track, some distance from the starting point and slightly up from the *finish line* banner which hung above the road. I could see Mort had found his position on the same side as the carnival grounds, so Duke and I worked our way through the crowd up to the barrier rope. Casting sidelong glances along the way, we spotted various cash exchanges going on around us.

Duke tapped me on the shoulder.

"Just ignore all the betting," I told him. "You know the old maxim, *what we don't know won't hurt us*. Besides, I have my own wager with Mort."

But gambling wasn't what Duke wanted me to notice. Looking off to his left and down the road, he pointed to the starting post. "We're just in time."

A flagman directed our two racers into position, far enough apart so he could safely stand between them.

My car was embellished on both sides of its long hood with the name of my company, *Gannon Fine Meats*. On the hood of the second car, Mort displayed his company logo *Silver Suds Soap*.

Humph. My friend Mort—a competitor through and through. His car had the better paint job. He had to outdo me in every way he could.

The drivers revved their powerful aircraft engines.

Verrroom! The thunderous sounds echoed up and down the road. And as the engines roared to life, so did the crowd.

"Yeaahhh," the nearly all male crowd reacted with animal-like cheers and hundreds of fists high above their heads, either waving their hats or pumping the air as the engine noises stirred them.

Our men were not just professional drivers. They were also entertainers who knew exactly how to please the crowd, allowing the spectators to feel the energy and hear the roar of two mighty machines.

To insure public safety, deputies kept the crowds corralled near the starting point and behind the dirt shoulders on both sides of the road. The spectators naturally pressed closer toward the road to get the best view possible, making it difficult to breathe with all the surrounding body heat.

"Dang, if this ain't the hottest afternoon air I ever felt!" a ragged onlooker shouted inches from my face. He was unshaven, missing several teeth, and hadn't brushed the ones that were left.

I fanned the air by my nostrils, hoping to redirect his rude breath.

"Ha! Guess ya ain't familiar with our Santa Anas," he said with a blowy laugh. "Ya can't fan y'self cool, cuz it's like wavin' your hand in a blazin' oven."

Duke and I moved toward a more open space and stood next to a young boy of about eight or nine. He appeared to be alone except for his white terrier with a big brown spot on his face. My well-endowed belly tended to bump into everyone, so standing by the small lad would seem to cause me the least amount of discomfort—I assumed.

His pet sniffed suspiciously around my ankle.

"Hey, hey!" I nudged the dog away with my foot. "Not on my leg you don't!" Maybe this new location wasn't as perfect as I thought.

"He just wants to meet you." The boy picked him up. The excitable dog squirmed in his arms. "His name's Spike, and I'm Howie. He's really nice once you get to know him, but I can hold him if you're afraid."

"Oh, no, that's not necessary, especially on a hot day like this."

And it was stifling. I wanted to remove my jacket, but instead I poked a couple of fingers inside my stiffly starched collar to let out a little heat. Clothing decorum had trumped my common sense, but I would not suffer much longer. Once the winning ceremonies were over, I'd rush back to my ranch and jump into our swimming pool before our guests would arrive.

Spike was glad to be back on the ground where smells abounded, but managing the dog was difficult for the young boy.

"I think it would be wise if you kept Spike tethered tightly on that leash you got there."

"Okay—wanna pet him?"

"Sure, why not." I bent down and realized Spike was indeed a pleasant little canine but extremely high-strung.

"You can pet him, too, if you like," Howie said to Duke.

Duke obliged, though it only encouraged the terrier's excitable nature with yaps and spirited jumps that begged for more attention, and not just a couple of bounces. The little dog jumped continuously, as if he had found a lost friend.

Again, our drivers revved their engines. They knew the spectators were anxious to see the two mechanical tigers unleashed in a fury right before their eyes. Speed, danger, and unbelievable risk were all parts of the day's excitement.

I looked at my watch—five o'clock on the dot, and the countdown had begun.

Duke and I focused our attention on the flagman whose black and white flag was raised high above his head.

Whoosh, down it went.

Both cars accelerated quickly, releasing large contrails of bluish-black exhaust. No doubt nearby spectators could use Mort's laundry and personal hygiene products after witnessing the official start. This gave scoffers ammo to claim the race was only a mindless publicity stunt.

Publicity stunt?

Of course it was, although its purpose was not to soil clothing. Boosting brand recognition in the greater Los Angeles area had become a secondary goal to our sporting obsessions.

And, come now, mindless?

How insulting to all of the fans who marveled at the exhilarating exhibition of speed and engineering.

"You've got an early lead, Phin!" Duke shouted.

"Yes, yes, I see!" I shouted back. I had an expectation of winning because my driver Jimmy Green had won several more titles than Mort's.

As cars roared past Duke and me at speeds of 100 mph, my heart raced right along with them.

"Go, Jimmy, go!" we yelled, causing the dog to join our unrestrained enthusiasm.

We were, by no means, the loudest voices in the crowd, but with the help of Spike we were possibly the most noticed persons.

"You can do it, Jimmy!" I yelled even louder, not that my driver could hear me from such a distance away or above the noisy engines, but as usual, I got caught up in all of the excitement. I felt like I was driving the car. Our competitions always made my adrenalin surge as if spurred on by an exotic drug.

With my attention sharply focused on the race, I watched Jimmy hold a slight lead. The roar, the smells of spent fuel, and the moving air compounded the thrill. Even the brazen little dog was caught up in the excitement—tugging hard on Howie's leash. These were two cars Spike desperately wanted to chase.

We stretched our necks and leaned over the barrier rope to watch the most dangerous part of the race—rounding the oil derrick.

"Here," Duke said. "Use my binoculars. They're much stronger."

"I didn't dare blink through the large lenses, as my driver managed to increase his lead substantially before starting into the turnaround. Jimmy fishtailed when he circled wide, stirring up a thick cloud of dirt that obscured Mort's car.

"I've lost sight of both cars," I shouted. "They're completely hidden by dust."

The crowd stood motionless, anxiously awaiting the outcome of the treacherous turn.

Jimmy emerged first from the cloud, and shortly thereafter, Mort's car, too. Both safely rounded the derrick, but the turn gave Jimmy a greater advantage by several more lengths.

They were in the final stretch on the public straightaway when I began to realize the victory was all mine. Jimmy's ever increasing lead would make him the inevitable winner.

"Come on, Jimmy! Step on that gas!" I yelled. "Don't lose it now!"

"You've got it, Phin!" Duke shouted. "It's all yours!"

But when Jimmy's car was about 100 yards from us, the dog jerked free from Howie's grip and dashed, rope still attached, toward the oncoming cars.

"Spike!" Howie screamed, running onto the track and after his dog.

Duke immediately intervened, ran after Howie, scooped him up, and bolted across to the road toward the carnival.

My driver spotted the two in the road and slammed on his brakes. I could smell the burning rubber. He skidded toward the spectators on my side, just as Duke and the boy plowed into the opposite crowd with a rolling dive.

In a remarkable display of driving expertise, Jimmy managed to avoid all of the people along the sideline by a nerve-shattering couple of feet—his car partially on the dirt shoulder.

I held my breath for a few moments while trying to comprehend the crowd's horrifying reaction. To my great relief, no one was hurt, but it was close—too close. And yet the race was not over. Several yards from the finish line, with no forward motion left, Jimmy turned back onto the paved road. He quickly accelerated, but it was useless. Mort's driver barreled down the road, passing Jimmy on his right, to cross the finish line first.

I was stunned.

By saving a child's life my driver allowed Mort to win—again. This was supposed to be my victory and my chance to rib my good friend. How could this have happened?

There would be no first place celebration for me tonight at the ranch. It would be just another Gannon Gala, and my humorous victory speech would have to wait for another time.

After the drivers parked their cars under the finish line banner, I walked over to Jimmy and was soon joined by Duke and Howie.

Duke and I coughed on the fumes that still hung in the air, but Jimmy sat quietly in his seat looking bitterly disappointed. Not all race car drivers were lucky. Many accidents and a few fatalities had been reported in recent months, but none had ever involved a child in the roadway—truly an upsetting moment for all concerned.

"Are you okay?" Duke asked Jimmy.

"Yeah, but how about you? That was some quick thinking on your part."

"Not a scratch on me or the boy."

Spike was fine, too. From out of nowhere, he jumped into my arms. I wanted to strangle the little beast, but there were cameras all around.

"Take off your goggles," I said to Jimmy. "Stand up. Let's show the crowd everyone's fine." I handed him the dog. "I promised excitement, and no one's going home disappointed." I put some folded money in Jimmy's shirt pocket. "Here, this is yours. It wasn't your fault you lost. You clearly earned your victory bonus."

With Spike eagerly licking Jimmy's face and Howie by Duke's side, we faced the fans on both sides of the road. It was a happy ending to what could have been a real tragedy. Although Mort's car finished first, Duke and Jimmy were the true heroes of the day and were rewarded with a thunderous applause. What an exciting Saturday afternoon, though I never liked it when Mort won. It made me compulsive about dreaming up a better comeback.

As I stood in the middle of the road, admiring the crowd's terrific response, I began to cough again. Only this time it was more of a wheeze. I thought, perhaps, it was a bit of dust in my throat but soon realized that wasn't the cause. There was more to my discomfort. The dry desert wind usually evaporated perspiration so fast, there was no need for a person to wipe it dry. However, I was mopping my face with a handkerchief.

"Ya okay?" Duke asked.

My cough subsided.

"I'm fine. Just help me walk over to the winner's platform so the photographers can take pictures of Mort and me for the newspapers. That's why we're here, isn't it—publicity?"

"Yeah, I hear you, but you really don't look so good. You've lost your color."

"Nonsense. I've lost nothing but this blasted race! I'm fine."

"You might believe that, but I don't," Duke said, serious but calm.

His skepticism was well founded. I knew something was wrong. I had to hold onto Duke's shoulder for balance as we walked over to the podium.

"Congratulations," I said to Mort over an orchestra of snapping cameras.

Newspaper photographs always seemed to amplify our contrasting physiques, which were once described by a journalist as akin to Stan Laurel and Oliver Hardy.

"Will there be a rematch, Mr. Cunningham?" one reported called out.

"Absolutely," Mort said proudly. "I had nothing to do with the dog's interference, and a subsequent race will confirm my car's tremendous power."

"How about you, Mr. Gannon? Will there be another race?" a second reporter asked.

"In light of today's events, I'm not prepared say there will be another race, but I can say there will be more Gannon-Cunningham contests," I replied.

As Mort and I posed for the traditional grip and grin photographs, he said to me with a wink and a wide smile, "We sure gave 'em a good show this time, didn't we?"

"Yeah." I rolled my eyes, disappointed to lose my $200 bet—now $400 in the hole. I did manage a strained smile while posing for additional publicity shots.

"I'm going back to my ranch with Duke," I said to Mort. "Do you mind staying behind and talking with the reporters?"

"Of course not. Go right ahead—we'll carry on."

"Thanks. Don't forget to send the pitchmen home with their pay, and make sure our drivers are invited to the party. My wife has promised a grand buffet."

Mort nodded, and as we left, I could hear him extolling the virtues of car soap.

After returning to my Cadillac, I asked Duke—voice shaky, "Would you mind driving? I feel a little dizzy in this heat."

Duke stared directly into my eyes. "You bet I'm driving, and we're heading straight for Doc Burton's."

I grumbled. "Never mind the doctor. All I need is a cool dip in my swimming pool."

"Let me put it this way, Phin. You look so bad that if you were a mirror, then I'd swear I was dead."

I paused a moment and took a deep breath. Inhaling was painful. "All right—have it your way."

While riding in the car, I felt nauseated, causing me to wonder if I were having a stroke. A person surviving a stroke was often left disfigured and unable to speak, or drooling out of one side of the mouth. A pitiful sight to be sure, and one I wasn't prepared to experience. Worse yet, maybe I was having a heart attack. Or dying? I didn't want that. I had often asked God to show me new and exciting places, destinations where a fifty-four-year-old would love to explore—someplace full of adventure and fascinating wonders. I just didn't expect a trip to heaven would be His answer—at least not today. I had too many things left to do here on earth, places to explore, cultures to experience, and most certainly races to win. Where did the time go?

I met Duke while playing baseball in Los Angeles back in the mid 1890s. I had an insignificant professional baseball career and was dropped from the roster at age twenty-one, but Duke threw an incredible speedball that made him a star athlete. His career was long for a pitcher—almost forty when he retired. That was when he became a bailiff at the Los Angeles County Courthouse. What a popular guy he turned out to be. Fans on occasion still asked him to sign their autograph books.

After my failed baseball attempt, my father, a cattleman from Downey, approached me with the idea of cutting out the middleman and selling choice cuts of beef directly to local meat markets, restaurants, and hotels. He recognized that as the ever-increasing populations continued to spill out beyond municipal boundaries, grazing land around Los Angeles would become more difficult to find. Our Downey ranch, now surrounded by developments, was too small to pay all the expenses. Should Father's new business model work, we would not need a larger herd, and if we should do exceedingly well, we would have the means to acquire more real estate in outer lying areas where grazing land was abundant and cheap. We started *Gannon Fine Meats* about that time. My partnership with Father taught me a lot about life and business and produced many fond memories of struggle and triumph with him by my side.

At first we were a small operation, working from our ranch, but after countless long hours, we were able to hire more people and open a slaughterhouse next to the rail yards in Los Angeles. The business grew substantially. Then one day, immediately after father's passing, the company became mine.

Mort's career took off once his father made him vice president of their family business *The Silver Suds Soap Company.* One of his first achievements was a new line of soap he introduced, *Sterling Pure,* which built up the family business on an image of purity and decency. Mort was a marketing genius. He could make customers feel dirty just for considering another brand. Then, two years ago, when the family business went public, Mort became president, and his father took over as chairman of the board.

We both possessed good business sense. Mort was able to grow Silver Suds into the largest soap company on the west coast, and I was able to keep Gannon Fine Meats strong and viable, maintaining our honorable brand name.

Dr. Donald Burton's office was a mere fifteen minutes away—a great relief because I felt weak and uncomfortable.

"You're in luck," Duke said as he parked in front of the doctor's house. "Doc's car is in the garage, which means he's home."

That was reassuring, though I was starting to feel better—at least until I opened the passenger door. As I lifted my right leg out of the car, I realized I was weak and unsure how steady I'd be on my feet. Duke helped me out of my seat and up the walk.

"You don't look quite as pale," he said. "For a moment there, I was afraid I'd lose you."

"Horse feathers!"

I could tell my situation was quite unsettling to Duke, so I tried to put on a good front. It took a tremendous effort to climb Dr. Burton's porch steps. Donald's medical office had a separate entrance, but his wife Florence met us at the front door of their home and invited us in. Her insightful eye instantly saw this was not an ordinary visit, so she quickly ushered me into the examination room. Always exquisitely dressed and coiffed, it never bothered her to take on the role of nurse at a moment's notice.

"Can you tell me what's going on?" she asked.

"I think it's my ticker."

"Then perhaps you should undo your vest and shirt while I fetch Donald. He's in the backyard and won't be long." Florence left, closing the door behind her.

The exam room had just enough space for the table, a tall medicine cabinet, and a small writing desk. Its only window was as large as the door and looked out onto the rear garden, where I could see Donald walking toward the house. While sitting on the edge of the table, I reached for the *Holbrook's Magazine* in the wall-mounted rack. I scanned its pages until a particular sports article by Travis Maxwell caught my attention. It was about a Lakota baseball team from South Dakota. The phenomenal players, obviously in their late twenties, had been a team since they were young boys, so the article stated. And although all of their competitions were held on their Pine Ridge Reservation, the renowned reporter claimed they played like Major League pros.

The strapping players were originally coached by a talented Catholic priest on the reservation. It was there, during their formative years, they learned the basic baseball rules and techniques. Later, the team went on to play at the Carlisle Indian School in Pennsylvania where they shined even brighter before returning home to South Dakota. The reporter noted the players' incredible batting skills and their ability to turn double plays with great speed and accuracy. Hmm, I thought—a baseball team. Maybe I could own a baseball team? Maybe Mort and I could have competing teams?

I had only partially read the article when Dr. Burton entered the room.

"Well, Phin, what seems to be the problem?" he asked, buttoning his white coat. "I saw Duke in the waiting room. Sorry I missed your race, but I had an important follow-up visit at the hospital."

"I'm sorry, too. It was a real crowd pleaser, maybe too exciting for me, though. While watching the race, I experienced some tightness in my chest and began to feel faint. It was also hard to breathe."

"Shortness of breath?"

"Yes."

"I'm not surprised by all of this. How much do you weigh? Three-twenty? More? It would be easier on your heart if there were less of you. How old was your father when he died of a heart attack?"

"Sixty-four."

"Hmm—but I don't believe he weighed as much as you." Donald sat down on a nearby stool and wrote something on my chart. "Phin, you may think I'm rude because I keep telling you to shed some pounds, but it's for your own good."

I had previously heard the doctor's comments about dieting when I passed two-seventy and then the three hundred mark.

Next, he listened to my heart with a stethoscope.

"It doesn't sound good, but all I can do is give you some pills to ease your chest pains. It's up to you to lose the weight. I want you to have many more wonderful years, but what I see is a man in poor health with very little time left."

"How much time?"

"I don't know. I really don't, but it won't be much longer. Since your last examination, your heart has developed a very irregular sound. You probably experienced a mild heart attack today…maybe you've had others."

"So, what are you trying to tell me?"

"I'm surprised your heart still works."

Donald didn't need to give me the grim news. The facts were obvious. I had little time left. My stamina was not as strong as it once was, and in recent months my whole body acted as if it were slowly shutting down. But no matter my condition, I didn't want to live the rest of my life as if I were already dead. I wanted to live it with all the joy I had ever known, making sure I had loved enough, experienced enough, and completely forgiven all who had ever harmed me.

Donald looked me straight in the eyes in a concerned, professional way. "You seem to be taking this bad news well. Are there other matters you'd like to discuss while you're here? I ask this not just as your physician but also as your friend."

"Thanks, Doc," I replied with all the sincerity one could expect after being told I was about to kick the bucket. "I suppose there is something. I'd like to have this magazine article on some Indian ballplayers from South Dakota. The reporter wrote about them while covering President Coolidge's recent visit to the Pine Ridge Reservation. Do you mind if I rip out four pages?"

Donald shook his head in disbelief. "Here's my advice to you. I want you to cut back on your food intake, and it wouldn't hurt to do some light calisthenics like a daily walk in the park—nothing strenuous. Stop and rest whenever you begin to feel the slightest shortness of breath. Honestly, I feel like a broken record every time I tell you this."

Donald turned around to count out pills from a large jar he removed from his medicine cabinet, so I continued to read the article.

"I just got that *Holbrook's* in today's mail," he said, "but you can have the entire magazine if you like. Don't know when I'll get the chance to read it."

"It wouldn't seem right to take the whole thing when I only want this one article."

Donald placed a small cobalt blue vial with a cork stopper in my hand. "Then take this. It's your medicine."

I held the bottle up to the light. "It looks as though there are at least a hundred pills in this thing."

"There are, but use them sparingly and only when you're having chest pains. I also want you to stop by here in about a month for a follow up exam weighing a few pounds less, so lay off the extra food. Small portions, okay?"

"Whatever you say," I replied, ripping pages from the magazine.

~ Chapter Three ~

I thought about Dr. Burton's warnings and decided it would be wise to start a new food regimen—but not until after our evening gala at the ranch. Rich foods and lively parties were a Gannon tradition at the old place. Mother and Father would regularly throw barn dances and cookouts for friends and neighbors because their main house was too small. Then after I married and moved to Los Angeles, Father razed their small cottage and built the 2,500 square foot, Spanish-inspired house. He also built a bunkhouse, and though it had been years since anyone stayed there, it could sleep up to a dozen or so ranch hands or exhausted partygoers.

After my mother and father passed, I added a swimming pool and the pool house. Guests often enjoyed a swim and frequently took advantage of the entire pool facility. Maggie always made sure both the men's and women's dressing rooms were well stocked with swimsuits, robes, and towels.

Maggie and Mort's wife Jeanne, close friends, both preferred to skip the afternoon race and visit at the ranch while a cadre of caterers scurried to make the party come off without a hitch. Our wives didn't think much of our competitions, and as usual, they were glad when our latest race was over. Too much tension, Maggie would say, and Jeanne never wanted to take sides.

Our resident caretakers, Karl and Ruth Warren, had plenty to do. Karl stood by the fire pit and monitored the side of beef, while Ruth oversaw all the finishing touches on the tables set up on both the upper and lower terraces.

The Warrens started under my father's employment shortly after Mother died. A cook and a groundskeeper was what he wanted. He felt fortunate the Warrens were available with few family obligations, and I liked them so much that I kept them on as resident caretakers.

By the time Duke and I arrived at the ranch, Mort and our two race car drivers were already there, and not surprisingly, most of the reporters. What a publicity ham Mort was. He often joked about it, saying that he had added a codicil to his *Last Will and Testament,* instructing Jeanne to invite William Randolph Hearst to his funeral.

As usual, Maggie made sure several notable couples, including fellow businessmen and politicians, had been invited to our party along with all of our neighbors. We never knew how large the final guest counts would be at our soirees, but it didn't matter. We always enjoyed the company of friends and meeting new ones as well.

"Sorry about today's outcome," my race car driver said to me as I approached the long food table set up under a white canvas tent.

"I'm sorry, too." Jimmy had no idea how sorry I truly felt.

"This is some place."

"I'm glad you like it. Make yourself at home."

I didn't mean to brush him off, but my eyes were focused on all the fruits, cheeses, and plated tea sandwiches beautifully arranged in front of me.

"Is this where you live?" he asked.

"No, our caretakers are the only ones here full time, but they always keep the master suite ready for my wife and me as well as the guest room for company. Our primary residence is in Los Angeles. It's closer to my office." I picked up a plate and handed it to Jimmy. "Don't be shy. Eat to your heart's content. I always do." I laughed, patting my midsection.

As I mingled among our guests, I quickly tired. I spotted some empty chairs on the upper terrace under our large awning—a favorite place for Maggie and me. At the end of many days we often relaxed there and watched the evening sun cast a warm glow over our lower pasture. The ranch had always been home to me, although Maggie preferred Los Angeles. The stench of manure sometimes bothered her, but to me it was the aroma of rich profits.

I took a seat on one of the Adirondack chairs, holding a nearly full plate of little sandwiches—two less than usual to follow Doc Burton's advice. In the other hand was my lemonade. I sat alone, devouring most of my food, wondering whether I should tell Maggie about my heart condition. And if I were to tell her she was about to become a widow, when would be the best time? Then it struck me. I should have a word with Duke so he wouldn't spill the beans. I managed to catch his eye and signaled for him to come over by me.

"What's up?" Duke asked as he sat down on the adjacent chair. "Are you feeling okay?"

"Ugh, I feel like I've been wrestling with a bear. It's Maggie I'm worried about. I haven't had a chance to talk to her about my doctor visit, and luckily, she hasn't had time to ask me why we arrived so late to my own party."

"Don't worry, Phin, I won't say a word."

"Good." I touched Duke's arm so he wouldn't leave. "Say, Duke, while you're here, may I ask, what do you think of me owning a baseball team?"

"Is there one for sale?"

"No, but I thought perhaps I could start one from scratch and play some winter ball in Los Angeles."

Duke laughed out loud. "Are you kidding? We're in the middle of September. I doubt any slots are available."

He had a point. There were always a set number of teams in the Los Angeles Winter League. They limited the number of clubs to assure all the Major League players a game every Sunday until spring training.

"Have you thought about playing in one of the inland leagues?" he asked. "You might be able to find enough semipros around the country to make a decent club for Riverside or Orange County. I'm sure team slots exist there."

"Never!" I snapped back. "Those leagues are barely profitable. Besides, Los Angeles is where real baseball is played. If I'm going to have a team at all, I'd want them to play in Los Angeles. And if I can't have a team in L.A., then I see no reason to continue with this baseball notion of mine."

Although Major League pros were not required for club entry into the winter league, every Los Angeles club owner coveted the nation's top players. But as Duke pointed out, most of the top National and American League pros had already signed with the best and richest winter clubs in California, Cuba, or in the Deep South—very disappointing news to me.

"I suppose well-established and well-financed clubs had no difficulty hiring Major League stars."

"That's the way it works," Duke said. "Even if one were allowed to have an L.A. baseball team at this late date, it would be difficult to put a good one together. Start-up owners like you will find it tough to organize a full team of highly skilled professionals in September."

"But not impossible."

"You're correct—not impossible. Let's see." Duke took off his straw hat and scratched his head. "You'll need to assure the Los Angeles League that you're willing to hire a first-rate team, which won't be hard until they ask to see your starting roster. You certainly don't want to be short a couple of Major League pros when they pose that question. Your honor and reputation will be on the line. And then you should have three or four good men on the bench. They can be some of our local semipros."

"Duke, I have no doubt I can pull this off."

"I believe you. You certainly have deep enough pockets to put together a topnotch club—if the Major League players are out there."

"Would you look into this for me?" I asked.

"My pleasure. I was wondering when the baseball bug would bite you again. Tell you what, Phin. I'll call the league president tomorrow and find out how many team slots are left."

"I knew I could count on you."

"Where will you be Monday morning?"

"We're staying at the ranch. Mort and Jeanne are spending the weekend with us."

"Then I'll stop by here on my way to work." Duke gave me a suspicious look. "What brought all this on so suddenly?"

I reached inside my breast pocket and pulled out the magazine article. "Here, read this."

I waited patiently as Duke studied the pages.

"Indians? You want to hire Indians?" Duke asked.

"Mixed in with a few Major Leaguers, of course."

"If they'll even play with untested amateurs! Travis Maxwell's a reputable reporter, and he's done some decent sports writing in the past, but these Indians aren't professionals."

"So, what if they aren't? They play like them."

Duke stood up as if he were about to leave, implying he wanted no part of my Lakota idea. "It says in your article that the Carlisle Indian School in Pennsylvania placed a moratorium on playing against all professional baseball clubs, so there's no real measure of their talent."

"But Carlisle did that because Major League clubs were making the students irresistible offers and enticing them to drop out of school. Can't you see? That's the proof. If our nation's best ball clubs wanted to sign them, they must be great players."

"No. It means without a professional comparison, we don't know how good they really are. Look here, Phin. It's one thing for Maxwell to claim these Lakota men play extremely well, but the Los Angeles Winter League is an entirely different level of play."

"Nevertheless, I'd like to make them an offer, and I'd like you to be their manager."

"Now wait one minute! I don't know anything about these guys. And who knows? Maybe Maxwell exaggerated their skill level in order to write a good story."

"But you said he was a fine reporter."

"Yes, but this a long shot, and maybe it's no shot at all. You'd have a better chance of jumping over the moon than winning any Los Angeles game with these guys."

"But ah, what an interesting gamble! I'm thinking like a fan sitting in the stadium, eager to be entertained on a Sunday afternoon. This idea of mine has a vaudevillian or a P. T. Barnum quality to it. Don't you agree?"

Duke hesitated and gave me a smirk. "Look at it this way. It's one thing to put *your* reputation on the line, but it's something entirely different to put mine there as well. If you pledge to enter this team into the Los Angeles Winter Ball League, and they don't play well, then I'll be mud in the baseball world."

Though Duke was skeptical about this idea, he didn't object entirely. He returned to his chair, sitting way back with his legs outstretched. We were both silent for an extended moment.

"I've always wanted to manage a Los Angeles team," Duke said, placing his hands in his pockets. "But the last thing I want is to be the butt of jokes in the baseball world."

"No one will malign you. These Lakota players could be the next Indian sensation in athletics. Think of Jim Thorpe and all of the Olympic medals he won in 1912. He attended Carlisle, and the public hasn't forgotten his tremendous abilities."

Duke didn't seem the least bit impressed.

"Do you know what gives Mort and me the most pleasure?" I asked. "Risk. But not any risk, a calculated gamble—taking our time, measuring the odds, factoring in all of the unknowns, and developing a strategy. It can be the most thrilling thing in the world. So, why not take a chance with me on these men?"

"Huh?"

"I'm betting these Lakota players are just as serious and competent as Major League pros, and I'd be willing to send you out to South Dakota to scout them."

"I can't leave work for baseball, but you certainly can. If you're really serious about all of this, then book a Pullman compartment and head there yourself."

"You know, Duke, that's not such a bad idea, and it sounds like you're in. I knew I could talk you into this."

"Wait a minute. Before you get too excited, we need to know how good these Lakota players are. I'll also need some lead time to work with the men. That is, if they're worthy."

Duke was anxious to leave. I could tell he wasn't completely convinced, but I also knew I could talk him into managing my team.

He stood up and gave me a few parting words. "You'll need at least twelve players to make a bare bones roster—preferably an extra pitcher and two good all-around men. And it's important that one other player can adequately substitute for a catcher. But if Maxwell has stretched the truth one inch about these Lakota players, you'll have to hire the best available players before I'll manage any team for you."

"Agreed. Now, if you don't mind, would you please do me a favor and find Mort. Send him this way, but don't say anything about our baseball discussion. I want to be the one who talks him into owning a club."

"Hmm. Let me get this straight," Duke said. "You want me to keep my mouth shut with Mort regarding baseball and the Indians, and keep my mouth shut with Maggie about your health."

"That about sizes things up." I reached inside my coat pocket and pulled out a bank draft made payable to Mort. "See this? That feisty little dog cost me $200. Tell Mort I need to give him his winnings. It will motivate him to come quickly and gloat by my side. I so dislike losing to that man, but I think a good baseball team would make a great rematch—if he's up for the challenge." I smiled at Duke and finished the last morsel on my plate.

After Duke disappeared into the crowd, I spotted Karl wearing a bib apron covered with meat sauce.

"Hey, Karl," I called out. "Is that beef ready yet?"

~ CHAPTER FOUR ~

A short while later, Mort sat down by my side. It was our first opportunity to discuss the day's race—not that I was ever interested in postmortems after losing. My hidden agenda was to steer the conversation away from our Miller racers, and then, with a little nudge, convince Mort to have competing baseball clubs as our next competition.

Rather than living a vapid, boring existence, Mort and I relished our intense desires to compete. We were constantly trying to outdo one another with every sporting duel our entrepreneurial minds could imagine, and as we grew into old men, those urges for a good challenge never diminished. Though looking back on our lives, I could see that the joy of competition was one of the few things we had in common.

"Here are your winnings," I said, handing him my check.

He looked at it fondly and grinned. "This means I'm $400 ahead."

I always allowed him to dance on his victories, though losing tormented me.

"I haven't had time to tell you, but Maggie and I are delighted you and Jeanne are spending the weekend here at the ranch. All of us have been so busy lately that we haven't had much time together as two couples."

A server stopped by with a tray full of lemonade. "Something to drink?" he asked.

"Yes, thank you," Mort replied, taking one of the tall glasses.

"And I'll have another, too. Thank you."

Once the server left, Mort chugged most of his lemonade, leaving some ice. He then reached inside his jacket, pulled out a flask, and mixed some of its contents with his remaining drink. "Care for any?"

"No, thank you." I looked at Mort and saw the very same scofflaw and prankster that he was when we were young.

"Don't worry. There's more where this came from. I probably have the largest gin cellar in Los Angeles. It'll surely outlast Prohibition."

"That's remarkable."

"My cellar may be remarkable, but it's not as remarkable as a sober man. Cheers." He lifted his glass.

"Mort, have you thought about the road you're on and where it's taking you? We're getting on in age, and we're at a point in our lives when time and purpose matter."

Mort's happy-go-lucky smile turned sour. "Now, what brought all of this on?"

"I felt a little ill today, and it made me question many things. It made me wonder if I were to look back on my life, would I see footprints on a path of virtue and generosity or on a path of avarice and selfishness. Do you ever think about that?"

"Hey, you're much too philosophical for me. What I'd really like to know is whether you're up for a rematch with our Miller cars?"

"I apologize for my weighty thoughts. After all, this is a party, and it's a time for lighter topics. But to answer your question—I've given it lots of thought."

"No doubt the owner will want his cars returned right away," Mort said. "So, I guess we won't have much time to properly market a second race."

"You're right about the time constraint."

"And our straightaway course was not ideal."

"No, it wasn't," I agreed.

"The spectators were too close to the action, and the near brush with disaster could have cost us dearly. Can you imagine the headlines and the public relations mess we'd have on our hands if that young lad or anyone in the crowd had gotten hurt? You and I were downright lucky today."

"I was thinking maybe we should scrap any plans of a racing rematch and come up with some other popular idea."

"How about airplanes?" Mort quickly spouted. "Ah, but then, we both can't have Charles Lindbergh for a pilot." He laughed out loud.

"Hmm, airplanes, I hadn't thought of that, but I should like to keep them in mind for some future race."

"What did you have in mind?" Mort asked.

"I was thinking along the lines of some sort of true sport. Boxing would be fine, except an indoor facility would make it difficult to attract a huge crowd like we normally have."

"What about baseball?" he suggested.

"That's an interesting idea—two competing baseball teams." I was pleased and surprised Mort headed in that direction so soon. A baseball challenge would excite him more if he thought it was his idea.

"But it's not realistic," Mort said. "All the local cities have their semipro teams."

He was correct. There weren't any available city venues.

"Then how about Los Angeles Winter Ball?" I piped in with the idea.

Mort rubbed his chin. "Sounds interesting—the two of us scouring the country looking for professional baseball players for our separate teams. I don't know, Phin. National and American League players would be expensive. But on the other hand, winter ball can provide a decent stream of income, and I bet Duke could get us into the L.A. League."

"I'm sure he could, if we can fill our rosters."

"Then let's have competing baseball teams!" Mort declared.

"A great idea—count me in!"

As the afternoon slowly became evening, the cool ocean breezes pushed back the desert air, creating a most pleasant atmosphere. Friends invited friends, who invited other friends, and before long a large crowd of partygoers found their way to our ranch to swim, dine, and dance to the live music that filled the air.

We hired our favorite musicians. Their large repertoire always seemed to please everyone. And after meeting and greeting dozens of guests, I managed to pull Maggie away from her friends and onto the dance floor. "Come, darling, this party is for us, too."

I was deeply in love with my wife. Even after many years of marriage, holding Maggie in my arms and swaying to the romantic music still thrilled me. But while enjoying the tender moments on the dance floor, I began to tire in the middle of our first musical selection. I had to sit down.

"Maggie, I see a couple of empty chaises. Let's grab them and watch our guests having the time of their lives."

"Phineas, only one dance? Are you okay?"

"Yes, I'm fine."

Maggie knew better. Her brows were furrowed with worry. She noticed I was out of breath. So, curling her arm around mine, we carefully walked off the dance floor to claim our seats.

The fresh night air felt good as we sat and watched the foxtrotters bounce to a livelier tune under the soft lights which hung on strands around the perimeters of the two terraces, setting the tone for a gala that would last well into the night. Most notable was Maggie's handsome nephew Paul, who was flirting with an attractive redhead at the punch table.

Maggie's sister and brother-in-law lived in Chicago. Their youngest son Paul asked if he could live with us in California, so he moved west when he was only a teenaged lad. That was when I put him to work in my slaughterhouse. He was a hard worker, and after a few years, he was able to find himself an apartment and fully support himself on his salary.

"Who's that pretty girl over there with Paul?" I asked Maggie.

"Mary Johnson."

"Homer's daughter? I spoke to Homer earlier this evening, and he said nothing about his daughter being in the crowd."

"That's because you men were probably talking about golf or cars. I invited Homer and Claudia, hoping they would bring Mary."

Maggie was clearly pleased that Paul and Mary had found each other, perhaps a little prodding by Mrs. Johnson had helped. We watched from a distance as our awkward nephew appeared nervous and unsure around the lovely lady. Paul was so mesmerized by her beauty and charm that he kept filling several cups of punch, not realizing he failed to hand her a single one.

"Paul's a smart man, but he's no Rudolf Valentino," I said to Maggie.

"Oh, but Mary's so elegant and sophisticated. I doubt she would be interested in that sort of suitor. She's more inclined to desire an honest, hard-working man who has financial potential."

We continued to watch with great delight. Maggie and I both thought of Paul as a son more than a nephew.

"Phineas, I don't like staring, but don't they make a nice couple?"

"Yes, very nice, even though Paul appears to have no romantic experience. On the other hand, I wouldn't want him working at my company if he were too forward with the lassies."

"Honestly, darling, he manages your slaughterhouse. What chance would he have meeting any women there? A man in his twenties needs to find a nice lady."

"Especially a banker's daughter. Maybe it's time for me to retire and give Paul more responsibility. He'll eventually take over the helm, you know."

"I'd love to see you retire." Maggie's voice was sweet and her eyes needy. "You work too hard, and I can see the toll it's had on you lately. I want us to spend more time together, travel, take an ocean liner—see Europe. A long cruise would be so good for you and good for the two of us."

I could see the joy on Maggie's face and sense the excitement in her voice. It made me realize that my office was no longer the place for me. My wife was never demanding, but an ocean voyage appeared as if it were something she truly wanted.

My next thought—am I strong enough to endure such a trip? I didn't have the courage to tell Maggie of my failing heart, but with the grim reaper looking over my shoulder, she'd soon find out, and then we might never see Europe together.

"Maggie, I want to take that cruise!" I slapped my palms on the arms of my chaise. "By golly, I'm starting the process of retirement first thing Monday morning, but don't buy passage yet. Paul has lots to learn, and all of my managers will need time to adjust to their new boss. There's so much to teach him before we can set sail."

"And no time to waste, is there?"

"Not even a moment, although the news will probably shock your nephew. I don't think he was expecting this until he was at least thirty."

Reflecting on my earlier visit with Dr. Burton, I wondered how much longer I'd live. Promoting Paul a little sooner was something I had been seriously considering. Maggie was right—there was no time to waste, and it was truer than she knew. If it were possible, if my heath would allow such a European trip, I'd have to immediately roll up my sleeves and order my life. Of all the competitions Mort and I had conjured up over the years, I was now in the greatest race of my life—a race against time. I had to act quickly to train Paul. This would become my highest priority—although it was unthinkable to die without evening the score with Mort.

"I promise you, dear," I said to Maggie. "I'll talk to Paul. He's awfully green, though, especially with executive decisions, but to his credit, he's a quick study. Most importantly, he's an honest man and always tries to do the right thing, so I know he'll be a fine president someday."

"Someday soon, I hope," Maggie said, placing her hand over mine.

"Yes, it'll be soon, and then you and I will voyage across the ocean on our romantic European cruise. I can't think of anything I'd like more."

Maggie leaned over and kissed me on the cheek.

~ CHAPTER FIVE ~

On Monday morning Mort and Jeanne joined Maggie and me for breakfast on our front porch which faced the warm early sun. Pink bougainvilleas, sweet fragrances from our eucalyptus trees, and soothing sounds from our fountain surrounded us.

I sat across from Mort and thought about how much we had aged. He was nearly bald but had a well-toned body for a man over fifty. I, on the other hand, had no admirable physical qualities other than a thick crop of hair.

His wife Jeanne was a socialite from a prominent family, practically handpicked by Mort's parents to be his bride. After some of Mort's dalliances with show girls, it prompted them to elevate their son's taste in women. I liked Jeanne. She was sweet and kind. And although her overall appearance was plain, she had been a good mother to their two sons, who were both away at college. Best of all, she had been a stabilizing influence for my friend.

"This certainly has been a grand weekend," Mort said. "Last night was just as fun as Saturday's party. After all those hands of bridge, what time did we finally get to bed?"

"Midnight," Jeanne replied.

"Phineas and I had a wonderful time as well," Maggie said. "We must spend more time together, like old times."

Jeanne smiled and took a sip of coffee. I noticed she was not her usual self, full of life and overflowing with humor. This morning she seemed somewhat standoffish.

"I do love your ranch," she said. "It's beautiful and quiet. And you're right, Maggie. We need to spend more time together. You and Phin must join us on Catalina next summer. We haven't had the opportunity to use our place this year." She turned to Mort. "What do you say, darling?"

"Sounds like a great idea," he replied. "Though it will be difficult for me to get away from work, now that we're about to build another soap factory."

"Mort, of course you can find the time," I said.

Our conversation was interrupted when we noticed Duke's Model-T turning off the main road and coming up our long driveway.

I looked at Maggie and then at Jeanne. It was time for Mort and me to confess that we were planning another competition.

"Ladies, what would you say if Mort and I owned competing baseball teams?"

"You're asking us to share our thoughts on your gamesmanship?" Jeanne said with a pleasant laugh.

Maggie's big blue eyes widened. "I'm surprised you came up with another competition so soon. Why, it hasn't even been forty-eight hours since your race car challenge."

"Duke has come with news about the Los Angeles Winter Ball League," Mort said. "We're about to learn if they'll grant us permission to enter our baseball clubs this year."

"Good morning," Duke called out as he walked up to the house.

We knew he was in a hurry because he left his motor running, but that didn't stop Maggie from being a gracious hostess. "Good morning, Duke," she replied. "Would you like a cup of coffee or breakfast?"

"No, thanks. I've gotta get to work. But first, have you seen the morning paper?"

"No," I replied.

Duke showed us the sports page. Its headline, *Another Save by*

Baseball Hero Duke Maner, was accompanied by a large photo of my driver holding Spike and smiling wide with Duke, Howie, and me in close proximity.

"I see they got a good shot of your race car," Mort grumbled. "That's a sneaky way to get your company logo in the paper. I should have had the great Duke Maner and the dog pose with my car and driver."

"What does the caption say?" Maggie asked.

Race car driver Jimmy Green, racing for Gannon Fine Meats, loses the race but spares the life of a young lad and his dog. Not only were the crowds treated to a demonstration of speed and engineering, but also of remarkable driving expertise.

Mort sneered. "Is that the only picture?"

"Yep," Duke replied. "The main story does say Silver Suds Soap won the race, but that's not why I'm here. I found out some good news and some bad news about the winter league."

"What did you hear?" I asked.

"The good news is the league is not full, but the bad news is they can only absorb one more team. The season starts the third Sunday in November, and if both of you men wish to enter a club, the league president suggested your teams have a playoff game on the prior Sunday. The game's winner can have that last slot. He mentioned Fiesta Park's ball field is currently available that Sunday, but it won't be for long."

"That's something I'd like to think about," Mort said, "especially since the losing team won't be able to finish the season."

"Yep. That's the disappointing consequence for the loser." Duke slapped his palm with the folded newspaper. "But unfortunately you can't wait on this decision. The league president is holding the field and needs an answer immediately. I thought I could tell him something this morning."

Duke looked at Mort and then at me, pressuring us for an answer. "Keep in mind, the Los Angeles League will expect both of your entries to be first-rate teams. And I gave him my word that both of you are financially capable of hiring the nation's finest ballplayers."

"We won't let you down," Mort said.

"I hope not," Duke replied. "The president is doing you favors by letting you compete for that last league position."

"Tell me, Duke, where could the losing club play?" Mort asked.

"I suppose they could join another winter ball league around the southland. Most will accept additional ball clubs, even after the season starts. But don't expect to recapture your costs, though you might be able to break even."

Mort and I stared at each other and grinned.

"Okay, I'm in," Mort said, and we cinched the deal with a handshake.

"Duke, tell the league president to schedule a game between Mort's club and mine on the Sunday before the season."

"Okay, but realize it means you gotta have teams ready by then."

"I shall," Mort replied.

"This game is gonna be one exciting challenge to watch," Duke said.

I concurred, imagining my Lakota players squeezing out a narrow victory, becoming a headliner in the daily newspapers, and surprising the sports community.

"Well, I've gotta go," Duke said. "We'll talk more about this later."

After Duke left, Jeanne asked, "Are you gentlemen still interested in our opinions of this new competition?"

The two ladies laughed as if it were their long running joke between them.

"Don't worry," Maggie said. "Jeanne and I are grateful our thoughts are not required."

"Then, I'd say we've had a terrific morning," Mort said. "Would you ladies care to join us for a walk?"

"I'm not interested in walking anywhere on this ranch," Maggie said, "unless Pork Chop is securely tied in his pen."

"He was fine during the party, entertaining his lovely cows behind the barbed wire on the lower pasture," I reminded her.

"That bull scares me to death," Maggie said firmly. "And all to his satisfaction, I'm sure."

"When did you get a new bull?" Mort asked.

"A couple of months ago. I get a new one every other year. Eventually, this ranch will disappear to the ever-sprawling city. Even now there aren't more than twenty head here, but I needed a new bull, so I bought Pork Chop from a cattleman over in Olinda. New bulls can be a little testy when they first arrive, so Maggie dear, if it will make you more comfortable, Karl could…"

"That's not necessary. I think I'll just stay behind, do some needlework, and visit with Jeanne."

"Suit yourselves, ladies."

Mort and I excused ourselves and headed behind the house toward the barnyard. I couldn't walk as fast, so Mort slowed his pace, which gave us more time to chat. Our busy lives had kept us apart for most of the year, though I saw him now and then at the country club. It seemed rather odd that we hadn't played a round of golf together in several months, and for the entire weekend we barely had time alone.

"How's the soap business doing these days?" I asked.

"It couldn't be better, but that's just my opinion. Our shareholders aren't so happy with some of my decisions. Their dividends this year will be much less than previously forecasted due to a land purchase we're about to make and some budget overruns on our new factory we're about to build."

"Budget overruns on a building you haven't even started?"

"Structural details we hadn't considered—most of the blueprints had to be redone after I fired the first architectural firm. But this new plant will quadruple our output once it's in full operation."

"That's quite an aggressive expansion."

"Of course it is, but I want to go national with our brand. For a few weeks there, I thought I was going to lose my job, trying to convince the board this is the right thing to do. But with a little friendly persuasion, the shareholders eventually saw things my way. We must grow the soap business or be overpowered by our competitors." Mort stretched out his arms wide and declared, "Bigger is better!" His strong statement started a few cows mooing—all standing behind the barbed wire fence. "I should have those agreeable animals on my board."

We both chuckled at the cattle's odd sense of timing

"The best part is" Mort continued, "bankers everywhere are begging us to take obscene amounts of cash on credit."

"I tend to be reluctant about putting too much faith in bankers and economists. I'd rather ask another small businessman his opinion of the economy. He's the guy who watches public spending most closely, much better than some Ivy League financier or professor."

"I'm not worried. Our debt will be short term. I'm still in negotiations over the land acquisition, and I have several more meetings with our architects. We expect to break ground next summer so the new facility can be up and running by October of '29. We'll start with a Madison Avenue rollout of our products, and with powerful advertizing, I predict our creditors will be completely reimbursed by 1932."

"What if your bankers are wrong?

"Herbert Hoover will surely win the election, and he'll keep our economy strong."

"I'm just worried that you'll be stuck with a huge debt you can't pay off."

"Oh, Phin, must you be so negative? This is America. We're a mighty nation, a true economic force in the world—and you, my friend, are beginning to sound like my nervous shareholders."

"Watch your step here. It's a little steep." I pointed to the ground, as we continued down the path alongside the vegetable garden. "You know, caution is not a bad thing, though it seems to run contrary to your makeup."

"You're far too conservative in business. You always have been," Mort said.

"I've always admired your colossal visions and your intrepid marketing that has made a fortune for Silver Suds, but I wonder if you shouldn't be more prudent now that your company has gone public."

"You can't be serious! Our public offering is financing our new factory."

"All I'm saying is—maybe it's time to temper some of your enthusiasm. It's no longer just the Cunningham family shouldering all of the risk. Lots of middle-class people are buying stock these days—teachers, factory workers, carpenters—and they're depending on your ability to weather economic downturns in the…"

I stumbled on the uneven ground.

Mort reached out and kept me from falling. "Are you okay?"

I didn't think Mort would notice my shortness of breath, but it was impossible to conceal. It was customary for me to take a walk after breakfast, but my fatigue within five minutes was surprising.

"I guess I'm a little out of condition."

"Then why don't we sit for a few minutes inside your bunkhouse? There's no one living in there now, is there?"

"No—no one," I replied. "That's a good idea."

Anxious to rest a moment and thinking of my Lakota players, I was eager to step inside. It had been over a year since I had inspected the building. Mort opened the door. The bunkhouse had no glass windows, only screened portals with wooden shutters that hinged at the top, acting like awnings when fully opened. With all of them closed it was dark, so we left the door wide open.

49

Mort pulled up a chair. "Here, have a seat."

"Thanks."

I took my time, taking deep breaths while looking around the room. Other than needing a good sweeping, the bunkhouse looked like it would be quite suitable for my Lakota team once all the bedrolls were uncovered and given a thorough beating. But regardless of its condition, I was grateful for the chance to sit for a while.

"Have you seen a doctor lately?" Mort asked.

"Yeah, I saw Dr. Burton, though I haven't told Maggie." I reached inside my pocket and showed him my blue bottle. "He gave me these and sent me on my way. It's really nothing to fret about."

"That's good. For a moment you had me worried."

"No reason for that. I just need to shed a few pounds. Seems odd to pay a doctor good money so that he can tell me the obvious."

Mort pulled up another chair and sat beside me. "I've been thinking about our baseball challenge and the importance of attracting fans."

I knew he was thinking more about promoting our baseball game, and less about my health. I could fall out and die, and Mort would still be chatting away about a rematch. But he was absolutely right about advanced marketing. It was essential in making our competitions hugely popular. Every Gannon-Cunningham race was blatantly sensationalized to assure massive crowds, with tens of thousands of "tickets" disseminated weeks before every event—all beautifully embossed and illustrated on both sides of post card stock.

Although our competitions were essentially free (they were always held in the open) Mort insisted on printing 25c on every ticket, along with both company logos and slogans. His idea of implied value had amazing results. What's more, our tickets were never collected, elevating their worth to souvenir status, a recommendation that we freely suggested to anyone wondering who would collect these fine pieces of paper.

Mort also liked to take our competitions steps further and send out notices to all the local newspapers, announcing that his company was actively soliciting ideas from the public at large for future races. The winner would be announced at the upcoming event and would receive several cases of his various soap products. It was all done to keep his Silver Suds brand in the newspapers without paying for advertising.

What size is Fiesta Park?" he asked.

"I think it holds around five thousand, which means we'll need some strong headliners from the Major Leagues, or else we may not be able to attract more than two or three."

"Hmm, sounds like Los Angeles needs some creative sponsors. Do you think they'd allow us to print two or three thousand Cunningham-Gannon tickets to make up the difference?"

"Mort! Winter Ball tickets are 50 cents each."

"Not this time." I'm going to suggest that it's more important to fill the empty seats for our playoff game than worry about selling tickets. We'll supply the crowd, and they'll reap the profits through added concession sales."

I sometimes wondered about my friend. But on the other hand, he was quick to ask for opinions or feedback from Jeanne or from me when his marketing and advertising schemes appeared to rub up against the bounds of sound judgment, good taste, or honesty.

"It sounds as though your plan will discourage legitimate ticket sales if fans can get a free pass."

"Maybe," Mort said. "I'll have to think this through more carefully, but I certainly would want a full stadium when our teams compete for league entry."

"I agree, that would be ideal. Now all we need are two teams."

Mort and I laughed because we both had lingering doubts about finding a team, but our entrepreneurial spirits thrived on this sort of challenge.

"You know, Mort, I'm actually feeling much better now."

"Good. Then let's close up this place and rejoin the ladies."

After the Cunninghams left, I decided to spend the rest of the morning at the ranch and go to my Los Angeles office late in the day. Saturday's episode with my heart and the shortness of breath that I had been experiencing made me realize that I should slow down. I wasn't going to say anything to my wife about my visit with Dr. Burton, but I had no choice. Maggie found the medicine bottle in my jacket when she hung it up after the party. All weekend her lips were sealed, but my time of reckoning came immediately after the Cunningham's departure.

"Darling, the vial that I found in your coat pocket looked like it contained heart pills. Is there something you want to tell me?"

I hated when she sweetly batted her eyes when I was caught red-handed. I was forced to tell her about the dreadful episode before I was fully prepared. But telling her wasn't the hard part. It was seeing the look on her distraught face as she first came to terms with the fact that some day soon she would become a widow. She didn't cry, not even a whimper, though I knew she wanted to. She simply took my hand and said, "It's going to be all right."

As soon as I had a moment alone, I stepped into our library, closed the pocket doors behind me, and called my attorney Frank Simpson.

"Frank? Phineas Gannon. I need to talk to you."

"Good morning, Phin. Glad to hear from you, but you sound serious. What's on your mind? Is there something I need to know?" he asked.

"I'm not in the best of health, Frank, and to ease some of my legal concerns, I want to make sure all of my documents are in order."

"I'm sorry to hear about your health. Is this a new condition?"

"You might say, because the doc made it official and gave me the grim news. My ticker isn't doing so well, though I've often wondered about it."

"Let me get your file. Can you hold for a moment?"

"Not a problem." I gazed into the full-length mirror mounted on the wall. Through the glass, I could see the portrait of Maggie and me on the opposite wall above the fireplace. Oh, how much I had changed. I was now two people packed into one body, whereas Maggie had remained as lovely as that first time I laid eyes on her. It was at a dinner in Los Angeles, the home of mutual family friends. Maggie was seated next to me. That was when I realized the occasion was a setup. I didn't mind the behind the scenes scheming that went on in order to put us together, because before dessert was served, I was sure Maggie would be everything I wanted in a wife.

After dinner we strolled outside, walking down the street and then up the other side. She was taller than most women I knew, yet well proportioned. I was awestruck by her deep blue eyes that glistened like sapphires and seemed to naturally draw my attention. I thought about holding her hand, but that would have been too forward and assuming for a young man who had just met a beautiful young lady. What I really wanted to do was to kiss her full lips and touch her thick auburn hair, but what would she think? What would the neighbors think? It was summertime, and the sun would not set for a few more hours. I nervously imagined all of the neighbors peering out their windows. How silly my thoughts were back then. In the end, we both knew that we were right for each other.

Maggie and I had no children—though nephew Paul had become like a son to us. And now, after Doc Burton's diagnosis, Maggie's future was foremost on my mind. What would she do? What would happen to my business? Paul would eventually run the company, but he wasn't quite ready. This meant I needed to spend all of my remaining time training him to take over. He had to be able to keep Gannon Fine Meats a successful entity so he could support my dear Maggie and allow her to have anything her heart desired. My visit with Dr. Burton made me come to terms with my physical limitations. Fifty-four years of age didn't seem very old when there was so much more in life I wanted. I continued to look at myself in the mirror, which I filled from side to side. Maggie got two people for the price of one—something that she certainly didn't bargain for on our wedding day.

"Phineas," Frank returned to the phone line.

"Yes, Frank, what did you learn?"

"Your *Last Will and Testament* seems to be in order. Paul will take over as president of Gannon upon your death, and your personal assets, the house and the ranch will go to Maggie. Is there something you wanted changed?"

"No. Just make sure that Paul won't have any legal difficulties taking control of the meat company upon my death."

"I don't see a problem, Phineas. Is there anything else?"

"Actually, there is. I'm about to hire some ballplayers for the Los Angeles Winter Ball League."

"Baseball? You're going to own a team?"

"Looks that way."

"Lucky you."

I looked down at my desk calendar and made a notation. "My first game is the second Sunday in November."

I swiveled in my chair so I could face the east window that overlooked our garden. I could always think much better when looking outdoors. "I'll need some contracts drawn up and sent to the baseball club in South Dakota. I'll pay for their transportation, lodging, and food in addition to their salary and uniforms. The players will probably want to bring their own gloves, but if necessary, I'll provide all the equipment as well. I just need you to prepare a contract for me."

"You're asking these men to be in Los Angeles in just sixty days? It will take me some time to draw up the contract, and you'll also have to consider the time it takes to mail it, get the needed signatures, and have the contracts returned in time to send railway fare. I'm not sure that's possible."

"It can't be that hard, Frank."

"I'll do my best. In the meantime, perhaps I can find an attorney in their area who'll help us. It would be easier to send the necessary documents to another attorney who can get the signatures in a timely manner and coordinate travel."

"I agree."

"Where do these ballplayers reside?"

"Uh, hmm." I was silent while I rotated the world globe in reach of my desk until I found South Dakota. "Uh, Rapid City, I believe."

"Well, if you're sure, I'll contact a few attorneys there."

"Thank you, Frank. As always, you're very helpful."

After we said our goodbyes, I thought perhaps I should have mentioned to Frank that the ballplayers were Indians, and they lived on the Pine Ridge Reservation. But that would only make him think I was not only in poor health, but out of my mind as well.

As I hung up the phone, I could hear the pocket door rattle.

"Oh, there you are, darling," Maggie said as she entered the room. "Our bags are packed and sitting in the front hall."

"Then I guess we're all set."

"Good, because I have a garden club meeting later this afternoon."

"Maggie, you'll be happy to know that I just got off the phone with Frank Simpson. I took the first step necessary in order to promote Paul."

"Oh, Phineas, you are serious about retirement." Maggie scurried around my desk and gave me a kiss. "I'm so happy to hear that. I just hope Paul has enough confidence to take on his new job."

"I wouldn't worry about Paul, though a three-piece suit will feel much different from his slaughterhouse apron. Your nephew is smart, and I have no doubt that he'll soon get a grasp of his new responsibilities. I'd like to work with him for a while, and then allow him to manage the entire operation without any interference from me, just for a short time, that is."

"How much time?" Maggie asked.

"Oh, not long. Maybe ten days or two weeks. It will help Paul build confidence in himself while we're out of town."

"Out of town?"

"Yes. A little getaway—just the two of us. I thought about booking a Pullman compartment and traveling somewhere north or in the Midwest. That way I'm completely unavailable."

"And did you have a particular place in mind in the north or Midwest?"

Maggie's raised eyebrows tattled. Her skepticism was strong.

"I understand that President Coolidge was quite fond of South Dakota, and he recommended it highly upon his recent travels. The Lakota people seemed to like the president well enough to give him the name *Wanblee-Tokaha*. It translates Leading Eagle. So, darling, I do hope you'll join me. It will be a pleasant change of scenery for us—a quick trip out to spend a few days absorbing the culture, the landscapes, and maybe we'll get the opportunity to meet a few Indians before heading home. How does that sound?"

"It sounds as though you're mixing the meat business with our trip."

"No, darling, you can rest assured. There will be no discussions of beef, but I am thinking about scouting some baseball players." I showed Maggie the article by Travis Maxwell. "I'd like to explore the possibility of signing this team to compete with Mort's."

"Oh, Phineas." Maggie gently shook her head yet smiled agreeably. "I could say that I don't want you to go, but the simple truth is—I don't want you to go without me."

It was just what I wanted to hear, because I didn't want to go anywhere without my Maggie. Our remaining days together were decreasing faster than I wanted, so every moment was more precious than the previous one.

"My dearest, I knew you'd see the merit in all of this." I took her in my arms and held her close.

"Of course I'd see it," she whispered in my ear. "With your baseball deadline looming, there's no time to waste."

While we stood in the library wrapped in each other's arms, Karl loaded our luggage into my car. It was time to leave, so we said goodbye to our caretakers and headed home.

We motored toward Los Angles without saying much. It was about a half hour ride from our ranch. Maggie sensed that I didn't want to talk about my newly discovered heart disease, and she was right. I hadn't had enough time to fully absorb the final consequence of my condition. I knew she wanted to express her concerns and fears, but instead she politely kept the conversation neutral during our trip home.

"The countryside seems to be rapidly changing," Maggie said as she gazed out her window. "Since we left Downey, I've counted eight commercial buildings under construction and two new housing developments. It's amazing how prosperous America has become since the Armistice."

"I've been wondering if this is true prosperity or an economy based on false ideals. People are living beyond their means, spending wildly and investing heavily with borrowed money. There's an air of overconfidence that is difficult to understand. One would think this should be of concern to every banker, businessman, and stockholder, but even Mort has decided on an accelerated plan of expansion for the soap company. For his sake, I hope this economy remains strong."

"I, too, have a concern about Mort."

"Oh?"

"Jeanne believes he's having an affair, and she suspects that it's the reason why he's been keeping late hours and not going out socially as much with her. Have you noticed anything unusual about him lately?"

"You silly women!" I rubbed my freshly shaven face across my lips, knowing that my words were not the most choice. "Mort runs a large enterprise and is facing many pressures right now. With this new factory he's about to build, I can certainly understand why we haven't been out with the Cunninghams in months."

"More like a year, which is unusual because we've always been so close. This weekend was just like old times."

"That's true. You see Jeanne quite often, and I see Mort now and then, but you're right, we haven't had much time together socially or as a foursome. Why don't you ask them to meet us for dinner at a nice restaurant? Pick a time and a date. Work it out with Jeanne, and I'll talk to Mort. You'll see, and so will Jeanne. He's just a very busy man and certainly not having an affair."

~ Chapter Six ~

Our Los Angeles home on Carroll Avenue was where I carried Maggie over the threshold after our wedding in 1898. Rich with years of sentimental memories, we vowed never to move from our grand, three-story Victorian.

We arrived home shortly after one o'clock. Maggie and I sat for lunch, and then I drove to my downtown office on Spring Street. My personal secretary Jane Pierce was not surprised that I had come in so late in the day, especially after the big racing weekend and party.

"Miss Pierce," I said as I passed her desk, heading for my office. "I want you to call the plant and ask Paul to come over here at once. I need to speak with that nephew of mine right away."

"Yes, sir. Would you like to know about your morning calls?"

"Yes, of course, but only after you talk to Paul."

Perhaps the stress of running a business had taken its toll on me, because the moment I walked into my office and sat down behind my desk, I felt that I should have one of my heart pills. It was better that Miss Pierce didn't see me take the medicine. She would worry over me like an older sister.

I liked Jane. She was an honest woman, though not much to look at. I always despised hearing comments that compared her looks with that of a vulture and hoped that she would never be exposed to the harsh words. Unfortunately for her, she had a body that was much too thin and boney, not to mention her downward pointing hooknose that most assuredly deterred potential suitors. But Jane was as loyal and dependable as a good hunting dog, and I would keep her as long as she would put up with me.

Within the hour, Paul was in my office. Unlike the burly Gannon men of my family, Paul was tall and fit, and like his Aunt Maggie, he had a handsome appearance—dark brown hair and deep blue eyes.

"Hi, Uncle Phin. That was a great race, and what a party!"

"I saw you eying a young lady at the ranch—Homer Johnson's daughter, good stock from Whittier and a wise choice. It would be nice to have a banker's daughter in the family. What's her name?"

"Mary."

"Mary is a good name, easy to remember. Sit down, Paul. I've got something I want to discuss with you."

"Yes, Uncle Phin?"

"I want to retire—the sooner the better. Your Aunt Maggie and I want to get away, take a cruise, see Europe. That means I'm going to promote you from plant manager to vice president of the company."

"Do you really mean it?" Paul jumped up and leaned over my desk.

"Of course, I do, and soon after that I'll make you the president."

"President? Golly, Uncle Phin," he sat down, a bit dazed by the news. "I'm not even thirty."

"Ah, you're old enough, and you certainly know the most important part of our business, a quality product. It's a tall order, son, and there's so much for you to learn, but I think you can do it."

"Wow, I can't wait to tell Mary, that is, if you think that's all right."

"It's up to you. Since you started here nine years ago, I've been impressed by your work ethic. After I promoted you to plant manager, you've demonstrated a real concern for slaughterhouse cleanliness and meat quality. They're paramount to our meat business. Without a fine product, we can't claim that we are Gannon Fine Meats. A bad product defames my name, and that can never happen. So, you see, a first-rate plant manager is a vital part of our operation."

"Did you have someone in mind to replace me?" Paul asked.

"That's your job. You've had plenty of time to notice the men at the plant. Pick out a good fellow with a cheerful but firm attitude toward others. Surely there are two or three candidates who could be promoted to manager. You must select someone trustworthy who has a good eye for overseeing the operation. From now on, your work will be primarily in this downtown office and in the field."

"What does a vice president do?"

"We have twelve salesmen here. Your job is to oversee their work, record the sales, and send the orders to the slaughterhouse. It's a fine line estimating how many head each day must be processed, but that's what will make or break our operation. Overkilling leads to lost profits, and under slaughtering makes for unhappy customers. Do you think you can handle that?"

"Yes, sir!"

"Good. We've just begun a new quarter, so it will be interesting to see how well you perform when it ends on December 31. I want you to take control. Be the boss, come to me with questions, but don't come to me with problems unless you absolutely must. We'll examine your books at the end of the year and evaluate your progress then."

"Gee, Uncle Phin, I don't know what to say."

"Say, *thank you* and shake my hand."

Paul took it and shook it well. "Thank you!"

"Now, would you kindly ask Miss Pierce to step in here, please?"

"Yes, sir!"

"You should know that if you're ever unsure of a decision, ask Miss Pierce, or maybe it won't be necessary because she often interjects her unsolicited opinions anyway."

As Paul left my office, he was so giddy that for a moment I thought perhaps my decision was a bit premature, but then, I was that way when I was his age, yet fully capable of handling any job.

"Yes, Mr. Gannon?" Jane said as she entered my office, Paul right behind her.

"Miss Pierce, I would like Paul to have the corner office—the one that we're using for storage. Next, I want you to find out what that vacant office across the hall rents for and offer them twenty percent less."

"Twenty percent?"

"Yes, twenty. That may not be acceptable to the landlord, but accept his counter offer whatever it is. We'll need that new space for our storage."

"Yes, sir. Will that be all?"

"That will be all, thank you. Now, grab your hat, Paul. We're going to Long Beach."

"Long Beach?" Paul tossed me a baffled look that questioned my decision. "Why should we go to Long Beach so close to the end of the business day?"

"Humor me, son, and follow along. We're going to meet a very special couple. A good salesman knows his customers and should think of them as family."

"Would you like me to drive your Cadillac?"

"Not this time. We're traveling on the Red Car. To manage a good sales staff, you have to know their challenges as well. Almost all of our salesmen make their rounds on the Pacific Electric. Come, we're off to meet some favorite customers, Adolf and Lisa Ginsburg."

Paul and I caught the Pacific Electric to Long Beach, the electric trolley known as the Red Car that covered nearly all of Los Angeles County. As our bodies swayed in the wooden seats on the long ride south, I told Paul some of the things that made my father and me proud to proclaim that we were Gannon Fine Meats.

When I was about twenty, my youthful mind didn't think that I'd be anything but an outfielder, but baseball was a profession where hard work and strong desire weren't enough to keep a young athlete employed. The foundation of a successful baseball career was talent—raw, unabated talent. Every time a player stepped onto a field he had to perform at a level that would dazzle the fans. Although I was better than most players, there were many men much better than I, so before the end of my second year, I was asked to leave. Though disappointed, I soon discovered that the largest setbacks in life were usually followed by the most amazing opportunities. That was why tragedy and heartbreak were so affirming—because life moved on.

After my short baseball career, I went into partnership with my father. We both felt that the time was right to take the cattle business in another direction and start our own slaughterhouse business. Selling beautiful sides of beef was more profitable than selling the whole commodity at cattle auctions where we were at the mercy of the ever-fluctuating market prices.

At first, Father did all of the hard work along with a few of our hired hands. I was the salesman on the road, looking for new customers—mostly local butcher shops and large, upscale restaurants in the Los Angeles area.

We began our small operation at the ranch, but after a couple of years decided to rent a warehouse in Los Angeles as our slaughterhouse. It was a perfect location, next to the railroad yard, and as our business grew, we were able to purchase the building.

Over the years the company flourished. Then, around 1910, I began traveling to Long Beach in search of new customers. That was when I met Adolf. He was a special man who gave me a keen understanding of life, of friendships, and of goodwill toward others.

As the Red Car slowed, I nudged Paul. "I believe this is our stop."

We stepped off the car and walked a few blocks to Adolf's Butcher Shop. I knew he would be there, working hard as ever. He still lived above the shop with his wife Lisa, and as we entered his store, the tinkling sound of bells filled the room.

"Ah, ha!" Adolf greeted me with a smile, a handshake, and a friendly slap on the back. "It's been too long since I saw you last, my dear friend. Where have you been?"

"I have been away too long. Adolf, this is my nephew Paul Borden. I'm teaching him the business so I can retire."

He shook Paul's hand. "Those are big shoes you must fill." He laughed. "Stay for dinner tonight. I'll close up early so we can visit."

"We didn't intend to cut your business day short," I said.

He looked at his pocket watch. "Ah, I'm only closing a few minutes early."

"Then we would love to stay. Right, Paul?"

Paul was a good man and followed my lead. "Yes. It's very kind of you, sir."

Adolf locked the front door, flipped the sign over to *closed*, and pulled down the window shades. "Come this way." We followed him up the backstairs to his residence.

"Lisa, my sweet," he yelled halfway up. "Whatever you're cooking in those pots, add more. We have guests."

I saw Lisa's head above me popping over the railing. She was curious to know who would join them for dinner. "Well, Phineas Gannon, who would have ever thought."

When we entered their home through the kitchen, she greeted me with a kiss and a hug.

"Come, come," Lisa said. "This is such a wonderful surprise."

Lisa was beautiful—not so much physically. She was short, too round, and had the misfortune of having some unwanted facial hairs. But her wide smile could melt any man's heart, and her infectious laugh always lifted my spirits.

"Lisa, darling," Adolf said, "this young man is Paul, Phin's nephew, and some day he will run the meat business."

"Pleased to meet you," Lisa said with one of her beautiful smiles.

"We love your Uncle Phin. Come sit down. I'll set more plates. There's plenty to eat."

After Adolf inspected the hearty beef stew that was simmering on the back burner, we took our seats at the dining table and waited for Lisa to serve and take her place. Adolf gave the blessing, which nearly made me cry. He thanked the Lord for sending me, their angel, to be a part of their lives. Perhaps Adolf was a little overstated, but I knew he was sincere.

"Did your uncle tell you how I got started in the butcher business?" Adolf asked.

"No, sir, he didn't."

"I didn't tell him," I explained, "because it was you and Lisa who gave Gannon Fine Meats its great beginning into the Long Beach market."

"You're too modest, Phineas," Adolf said. "Let me tell you, Paul, what really happened. Lisa and I had only been married a couple of months when we decided to save our money and go to America."

"That must have been some time ago," Paul said.

"Oh, yes, but we won't go into that, especially because it seems like only yesterday. Like your Uncle Phineas, I was working for my father," Adolf began his story. "He was the butcher in our small village back in the old country. My older brother would some day inherit the family business, so I knew I must find another place to set up a butcher shop. I worked for several people and saved enough for steerage to America for Lisa and me. We had a little extra money to settle in California, but that plan would be delayed for a time. Before we boarded the ship to America, Lisa realized that she was with child, so we decided it would be best to stay in New York City until our dear Ludwig was born. I worked in New York a few years, saved some more money in order to travel to California. We had enough means to rent this Long Beach storefront, but not enough to compete with the other butchers in the area. Then one day your Uncle Phin stopped by our shop. He also wanted to break into the Long Beach market and sell his beef."

"For several months Adolf was my only Long Beach customer," I said with a slight chuckle. "I was no salesman back then. All the other slaughterhouses were slaughtering my sales pitches in the area."

"Gannon Fine Meats was the only company to give us credit," Adolf said. "We hadn't paid any of our bills in weeks. Our credit was kaput because our dear Ludwig was very ill. All the money was going to help our son."

"At least until a specialist diagnosed his condition," Lisa said as her eyes welled up. "Our Ludwig had an abnormal blood condition and would soon die."

Adolf looked at his wife, saw her pain, and continued the story for her. "But your Uncle Phin came to our rescue. He sent a man from his company to run the business for almost a month so that Lisa and I could spend those last days with our son—sometimes here but most times at the hospital."

"That was Charlie," I further explained to Paul, "one of our first employees when my father and I opened our new slaughterhouse. I got this bright idea that if I had to pay Charlie when there was very little work at the slaughterhouse, why not send him to Long Beach to run Adolf's butcher shop?"

"You were an angel sent from heaven," Lisa said, staring into my eyes.

"No, Lisa, the fact that I could help you and Adolf gave me immeasurable joy, and it worked out so well for the company. After a couple of days working at the butcher shop, Charlie told me there were no customers, so I decided to have the sale of the century. I ran an ad in the Long Beach newspaper that said, '*No purchase necessary!* FREE SAMPLE POUND OF FRESH BEEF, *until 5 o'clock p.m.*' Folks were lined up around the block. Most had never shopped at Adolf's place."

"It was brilliant," Adolf said, smiling as he reminisced. "People generally had no need for one pound of ground beef, so they bought one, two, or three pounds more, also buying steaks, sausages, chops, roasts, sauces, knives, seasonings, and anything else we had for sell.

By the end of the day when Lisa and I had returned home from the hospital, our cash register was overflowing with money."

"It was so fun, bringing in all of that cash," I said. "Charlie and I never worked so hard in our lives and loved every moment of our big giveaway!" I blurted out one of my deep belly laughs. "I was definitely the unexpected winner that day. The sign in the window claimed that Adolf exclusively sold Gannon Fine Meats, and after that successful day, our Gannon brand became a household name. From then on, my father and I were the beef kings in the Long Beach area."

I wanted my nephew to learn about Adolf and Lisa because it demonstrated our company philosophy. Father and I built our business by helping others whenever and wherever we could. Owning a business was a tough, competitive occupation that could harden a person fighting for position in the marketplace. As aggressive, unscrupulous businessmen pushed their way to the top, they often stepped over the carnage they left behind. Paul was too young and inexperienced to understand the importance of restraint. But I wanted Paul to know a better method of doing commerce and how to keep his heart from growing cold.

I learned through this experience that success smiles on the kind and generous entrepreneurs. Lisa and Adolf would never forget those final days with their son Ludwig, and I would never forget the immeasurable pleasure I felt by helping others—and not just Lisa and Adolf. Hundreds of people stopped by that day for their pound of beef. Most were there to take advantage of the free offer, but there were many waiting in line for a chance to serve a long overdue good meal to their family with that one pound of free beef.

Looking back at my life, I noticed certain events that became significant turning points. The wonderful day in Adolf's Butcher Shop was one of those times for me. From that day forward I realized that everyone had a story of lost hope, of pain, and of darkness, and we all had a duty to shine a little light, to be a beacon of hope for those in need until those disparaging moments passed.

I was sad that Adolf and Lisa had lost their little Ludwig. And like Maggie and me, they would remain childless. In time, we accepted our physical limitations and moved on with our lives.

~ Chapter Seven ~

Wednesday Duke stopped by my office, bursting with enthusiasm.

"I got in touch with Travis Maxwell through his publisher," Duke explained, "He told me how to contact Maxwell. And get this… He's in Hot Springs, South Dakota, not far from the Pine Ridge Reservation."

"He's still there?" I asked.

"Yep. After his feature on President Coolidge's trip to the Black Hills and his follow-up story on the Lakota baseball players, he was assigned to write one more article on the region for the next issue of *Holbrook.*"

"Did he tell you anything more about the players?"

"He definitely believes they play like pros." Duke picked up a baseball sitting on my desk and juggled it against his bicep. "I'd have doubts, except Maxwell has done a fair amount of sports writing. He noticed that the players were quite serious about physical conditioning, which is good. I suppose that's something they picked up at Carlisle."

"How about their pitchers? Did he mention them?"

"No, not a word. Ah, but Phin, I wish you could have heard the excitement in Maxwell's voice coming over the telephone wires about these ballplayers."

"How much longer will he be in South Dakota?"

"He's about to leave—filed his last story. Reporters can do that with ease these days. They dictate over the phone to a stenographer. But get this…if he knows you're coming, he offered to drive you to the Pine Ridge Reservation and introduce you to the Lakota players, though it'll mean that you'll have to leave right away."

"I can do that!"

"If that's the case, Maxell will delay his departure. He smells another story in this, maybe an ongoing series."

"I'll wire Maxwell today and tell him that Maggie and I are on our way."

"I wouldn't leave without contracts for those players to sign."

"Fiddlesticks with the paperwork. I can work out the details later. Besides, my attorney won't have anything ready this soon. Duke, there's no time to lose. Maggie and I are going to hightail it out there. Don't you see? This is great news. Ah, Mort's going to be shocked. I just bet you he hasn't even found one player, and here I might have an entire team!"

"Don't go thinking that far ahead of yourself. You might have a team, and you might not. You gotta analyze them carefully, and don't just hire them because they wear feathers. I'm not managing a bunch of sandlot players."

I put my hand on Duke's shoulder. "Don't worry, my friend."

I took the baseball from him and held it up above my head. "My only professional homerun and trophy. I may not have been as good a ballplayer as you, but I know good ballplayers when I see them. Where did you say I could find Maxwell?"

"Hot Springs. Hot Springs, South Dakota."

"Good work, Duke. Why, if I were several pounds lighter, I'd jump on this desk and swing from that light fixture! Morton Cunningham, I'm going to get the best of you this time!"

As soon as Duke left, I asked Paul to step into my office.

"Yes, Uncle Phin?"

"Paul, I know this is short notice, but your aunt and I are about to leave for South Dakota."

"South Dakota?" Paul's lower jaw dipped slightly. "What kind of destination is that?"

"We're going to retrace some of President Coolidge's recent travels there, which means we'll be gone as much as two weeks. And this, my dear man, will give you an opportunity to try your hand at running the company."

"So soon?"

"Ah, don't look overwhelmed. I know you can do it. Certainly an intelligent man like you can rise to the occasion."

"But Uncle Phin…"

"Now, stop right there. You're the new boss, and I want you to look the part. Feel it in your gut. You're from good stock and fully capable of this—and don't forget it. From this very moment until I board that train, I'm going to give you a crash course on becoming the chief executive. So, let's roll up our sleeves and get to work."

Before the week was out, Maggie and I were packed and ready to go. Miss Pierce, believing that our sole purpose for the trip was to give Paul a trial run as acting president, managed to book us a Pullman sleeper compartment and rearrange my schedule.

Paul had selected a fine man to replace him as the slaughterhouse manager, and after a follow-up inspection there, I realized my nephew had great potential. Best of all, the company had an outstanding sales staff to back him up, and if Paul should have any doubt about a major decision, Miss Pierce would not let him fail.

Paul drove us to the station and bid us farewell. I shook his hand before boarding the train and saw my nephew as the essence of satisfying a great responsibility, not just for the company but also in honor of my father. Paul was being nudged out of the nest and asked to fly. It was like an official passing of the torch from one generation to the next, a prideful moment that was most gratifying for me.

Once Maggie and I settled in our Pullman compartment, it dawned on me that during our twenty-four years of marriage, Maggie and I rarely vacationed, and when we did, it was often with other couples. Even though we were always together, my business and Maggie's charity work and social clubs kept us apart. How thoughtless of me. Why had it taken me so long to realize that Maggie had never put her desires first when they conflicted with my goals and dreams?

After sunset, we sat at a table for two in the first-class dining car while the train barreled through the desert. Over steak and potatoes, we reminisced about our honeymoon, the last time we shared a quiet week—just the two of us. We had rented an oceanfront cottage in Santa Monica, and for seven glorious days we were a carefree and blissful couple. Fit as a fiddle and looking much better in a swimsuit, I recalled the hours we enjoyed riding the waves, picnicking on the beach, and just being together.

"Darling," Maggie reached across the table and put her hand on mine. "I suspect you may not live long enough to visit Europe with me, so let's pretend that out this window we are seeing Venice from a gondola. And look, there's Notre Dame Cathedral and Buckingham Palace. Let's look out this window and not see the dark of night, but the sun rising over the Atlantic Ocean.

I was so choked up, I couldn't say a word. I closed my eyes gently, briefly, and then opened them to see my beautiful Maggie.

~ CHAPTER EIGHT ~

"I'm finally glad to put my feet down on solid ground," I said to Maggie as soon as we stepped off the train in Hot Springs.

"I certainly agree," she said. "A few days of feeling the sway of the train is quite enough for me."

We noticed a young, ruddy-faced gentleman on the platform heading our way. His well-worn suit and rumpled overcoat made him appear as if clothing were a daily uniform rather than a statement of style. But it was the pencil behind his ear and small notebook tucked in the band of his backward tilting hat that told me he was our reporter.

"Mr. Gannon?" he asked.

"Yes, so you must be Travis Maxwell, from *Holbrook's Magazine*."

"In the flesh," he said, shaking my hand.

"This is my wife, Mrs. Gannon."

"Pleased to meet you, ma'am." He removed his hat and smiled.

"My pleasure as well," Maggie replied.

"Then may I welcome the two of you to the front door of the Black Hills? *Paha Sapa* to the Lakota. If you like, I'll be glad to drive you to your hotel. Does the stationmaster know where to send your luggage?"

"Yes, thank you," Maggie said.

"That's good, because there are ten hotels in Hot Springs—quite remarkable for such a small town."

We looked around in all directions. Situated in the middle of nowhere was this very small town surrounded by reddish canyon walls—the same color found in the sandstone masonry used in the construction of the train station and most of the commercial buildings along the town's main street.

"Ten hotels—that is amazing." A sudden gust of wind caught the rim of Maggie's cloche hat, but she managed to hold it in place as she turned to look at the entire downtown area.

"Indeed it is, Mrs. Gannon. This area attracted many settlers during a gold rush in the late 1880s, but today Hot Springs is known for its healing waters."

"Really? What sort of cures do they offer?" I asked.

Maxwell chuckled. "Something for every sort of ailment, but nothing that I've been able to confirm. You might try plunging into its warm springs, sir, or taking a mud bath. Lots of people do. People come from miles away for treatments, so the water and the mud must do something for the body."

"Then I shall indulge myself immediately," I said. "It certainly couldn't hurt. Mr. Maxwell, you're quite the helpful gentleman, and I must thank you for your hospitality and for extending your stay here on my account."

"My pleasure, sir, but there's one thing you should know. I'm leaving South Dakota the day after tomorrow. I've been reassigned to Denver. But don't worry about the Indian ballplayers. They're expecting us tomorrow, although in order to meet these guys, we'll need to leave early."

"How early?" I asked.

"After breakfast. That will give us time to watch the men play some ball before we head back. If you don't mind, I'd like to return to Hot Springs before sunset. My Tin Lizzy is a reliable machine, but not being from these parts, I'd rather travel during the daylight hours while I can recognize the landscape and hungry varmints."

"My dear man, how can I ever thank you for your generosity?"

"It's easy. If you hire these Lakota guys, I'm going to write about your trip to South Dakota and to the reservation. With a successful sequel, surely my publisher will send me to Los Angeles to cover the winter ball season. It will be a great follow-up series. Don't you agree?"

"Absolutely. Everyone roots for the underdog. That's why I'm here," I said, thinking of Mort's reaction when my Lakota ballplayers scored a big feature in a national publication.

"Can you imagine the story!" Maxwell said. "What a sensation if these Lakota ballplayers overpower the best American and National League players."

He pointed toward the curb. "That's my car over there."

It was a Model T which appeared as if it had seen thousands of rough road miles. And although it had a canopy, it was essentially an open-air vehicle, which wasn't a problem on such a pleasant day.

He opened the passenger door. "Mrs. Gannon, may I help you in?"

"Yes, thank you."

"You may have the back seat," Maxwell said. "It will be much more comfortable for you."

I sat in the front, and the three of us rode a few blocks to the Evans Hotel—the car sputtering and backfiring all the way.

Almost immediately we spotted the hotel. The imposing five-story, red sandstone structure had a castle like appearance, and I marveled how a remote town in a remote state could have such a first-rate hotel. The massive structure was much wider than it was tall. Maggie was most impressed by the grounds that surrounded the hotel. They were impeccably groomed with lush landscaping. The hotel seemed to demonstrate the owner's faith in the future prosperity of Hot Springs, and for that matter, the entire nation. Its bold expectation of an unshakable American economy reminded me of Mort's perceived invincibility.

After Maggie and I said our goodbyes to Maxwell, we retired to our room. I had requested a treatment at the resort's health facility, so within minutes a personal clinician came to our room. We discussed my clothing needs, and then he escorted me to the hotel's spa.

"This way," he said as we walked down a long corridor toward the health facility and then to my changing room.

After disrobing, I was immediately immersed in a large bath of warm mud.

"This large tub reminds me of my one at home," I told the assistant. "Mine was manufactured by the same company that made President William Howard Taft's. I dare say, I'm similar in size as he."

I sunk down deep, feeling the soupy clay oozing though my toes, under my arms, and in the folds of my flesh until I lay in the tub up to my neck.

The clinician placed a tall glass of cool water within my reach. It was tightly wrapped in a linen napkin so it wouldn't slip through my fingers. "I'll be back in about thirty minutes to plunge you into our town's famous spring waters," he said. "They bubble up from the ground at about 90 degrees. It's all done in preparation for your deep muscle massage."

As I drifted off into a light slumber, I began to feel buoyant and relaxed, thinking that if it weren't for the Lakota ballplayers, I wouldn't be in Hot Springs, South Dakota, enjoying the quiet pleasures of their soothing minerals. And even though California had many fine mineral baths and spas in several locations, I simply had never taken the time to visit any of them, nor had I ever paused long enough to consider the need.

In the quiet and darkened room I thought about my future and about my twilight years with Maggie that I might never see. I began to think about what mattered most in my life. It was Maggie, her future, and her happiness. Our South Dakota trip showed me that I had been running faster than my body could endure. It was time to slow down, and in doing so, just maybe I could have a few more days with her.

~ CHAPTER NINE ~

The following morning, Maggie and I waited in the lobby for Mr. Maxwell, and it wasn't long before his car put-putted up to the front of the hotel.

"I believe your ride is here," the bellman said, stifling a grin. He opened the heavy door for us.

"Good morning, Mr. Maxwell," I called out to him.

"Good morning to the both of you," he replied, tipping his hat. "Are you ready to see the most sensational ballplayers in the Midwest, and who knows, perhaps the entire United States?"

"You sound confident about these men. That's good, but don't expect me to hire this team just so you can land a winter job in Southern California," I joked, while helping Maggie into the back seat.

We took off immediately, bouncing along a narrow dirt road, heading east-southeast at about 35 miles per hour. The air was chilly, but it wasn't cold. Just the same, Maxwell had lap robes available should his thin-blooded travelers require more warmth. And although we didn't need blankets, we did need to wear the goggles he provided, which we used for most of the trip to shield our eyes from the occasional burst of wind that kicked up clouds of dust.

"How long have you been in South Dakota?" I asked over the loud sounds of his car—*chuga, chuga, chuga.*

"As of now, eight weeks," Maxwell replied. "And I'll be glad to miss the Dakota winter."

"I don't blame you," I said. "I'm a native Californian—southern California, that is. Whenever I want to see the winter snow, I stand in the seventy degree weather and look off in the distance at the mountains."

As we continued along the rugged road, climbing and descending numerous grades toward the village of Pine Ridge, Maggie was curious about a certain matter. She tapped Maxwell on his shoulder to get his attention over the loud engine noise.

"Mr. Maxwell."

"Yes, Mrs. Gannon?"

"I noticed that you have a holstered gun under your seat."

"That's right. Davey Crocket may have killed a bear with his bare hands, but I'm a writer, not a frontiersman. Should we encounter any aggressive wild animals, it's a wise thing to have handy. Most of the beasts keep to themselves, but a rabid one may not be so polite. Don't worry, though, I haven't had the need to use it, and I doubt that I ever will."

"How much farther is this reservation?" she asked.

"It's about forty miles from Hot Springs, and we're not even halfway." Maxwell looked at his watch. "We should be there in less than an hour."

Satisfied with the answer, Maggie sat back and relaxed for the rest of the trip.

Continuing on toward the reservation, there seemed to be no end to the horizon, only miles of rolling, grassy hills, punctuated with buttes rising up from the ground.

Near the outskirts of Pine Ridge, several Lakota children had gathered. They watched us from a distance with great curiosity for our automobile.

"These young ones can hear my car from miles away," Maxwell said, "so they're usually waiting at this spot when I arrive, like a welcoming committee of sorts."

As we entered the village, I couldn't help but notice the hardships of this Oglala tribe. It was not sustained by free markets and capitalism but by government subsidies and the Catholic Church. There were mostly crude huts and some tipis where families lived. Only a few modern buildings had been erected, including a large Catholic school. Overall, the underdeveloped community was rife with poverty. It sickened me to see the people living in such conditions. We drove through the heart of the village, and a young man emerged, waving his hands as if he were looking forward to our visit.

"That's the team's captain, Bill Singing Wolf," Maxwell said. "He plays right field."

"He looks quite athletic," I replied.

Maxwell stopped the car and introduced us to Bill.

"The players are all waiting for you," Bill said. "We have about thirty men who would like to tryout for your team."

"Well, then, if that's the case," I said, "let's...*play ball!*"

I got in the back seat with Maggie, and Bill took my place in front, and we continued on toward the ball field, which was located near the school.

"Pull up over there," Bill said pointing to an area that was a short distance from the left foul line. "Your car should be safe from flying balls—no guarantee, though."

Maxwell laughed as he parked the car. "As if this old thing couldn't take another dent or two. Say, I hope you don't mind if I don't join you. I'd like to mingle with the players and get some of their thoughts about this tryout."

"Not at all," I replied. "You have a story to write."

Bill escorted us past hundreds of people sitting along the sidelines and then showed us our seats in the middle of a small, three-tiered, wooden bleacher—the only one for the field.

"Ah, reserved box seats," I said with a chuckle, and then helped Maggie climb up to the second row. To my right was an old man, a

Lakota tribal elder, whose face bore witness of many hardships. His deep wrinkles looked as though they were carved into his face, and he seemed to have difficulty seeing. Upon closer inspection, I noticed that cataracts had begun to form over his eyes.

"Welcome, my friend," he said. "I'm Amos Wise Heart, and you must be Gannon."

"Yes, sir, I am—Phineas Gannon, and to my left is my wife Maggie."

"How do you do," Maggie said. "I'm pleased to meet you, Mr. Wise Heart."

"As am I," he replied.

I wanted to be respectful of this Lakota gentleman, and so I wondered how I would address him. "Mr. Wise Heart, because I'm not from these parts, and because I'm more accustomed to urban ways, may I ask how I should properly address you and the other Indians? For instance, I should like for you to call me Phin because my friends address me in that manner."

"I'm honored to be your friend, and so I would like for you to call me Amos."

"Thank you, Amos. I'm also honored," I said, noticing something very curious about the elderly man's hair. It was parted down the middle into two long braids with silver crucifixes attached to each end. "Those are lovely crosses you have tied to your hair," I told Amos.

"Thank you. They were a gift from McKinley."

"President McKinley?"

"No, one of the Catholic priests on our reservation—McKinley." He pointed toward home plate. "That's him over there with the players."

Standing in the infield was a forty-something man having a few final words with the Lakota players. He appeared as if he could have been a very fine athlete at some point in his life.

"You wear the crosses, yet you don't address him as Father McKinley?

"How can a priest be a father, when he does not enjoy the scent a woman? Besides, my Father lives in heaven. McKinley lives in South Dakota."

"You have a point, there."

"He calls me Amos, just like the wise prophet of the Bible, and I call him McKinley."

"May I ask how you knew where McKinley was standing?"

"He told me where he'd be, and my vision isn't totally gone."

I became self-conscious as to how I was being perceived, but it didn't deter me from continuing my line of questions. "Amos, I hope I'm not being too blunt or offensive, but do you believe in the Bible?"

"Oh, yes. It's the Good Book."

"And about this priest…"

"McKinley?"

"Yes."

"He's very kind and a good friend. Taught our children to read, and he taught the boys baseball. Before these players attended the Carlisle School, they played well. McKinley has been good for our reservation. He reads the Bible to me everyday."

"To convert you?"

"I'd like to convert him. McKinley knows baseball, but not much about the unseen. That's why I help him with the scriptures."

"Oh, come now!" I was shocked that Amos would say such a thing. "A priest must be well versed in the Holy Scriptures in order to be ordained."

"He reads the Bible, but not with the eyes of a Lakota. Too bad he does not possess the wisdom of the Oglala. There is much more to the ancient words of the scriptures than what McKinley sees—very unusual for a spiritual leader not to notice. But he is still a young man, and I will continue to guide him as he reads to me."

"This is extraordinary," I declared.

"The words of the Book say it well, my friend, '*Seeing they did not see, and hearing they did not hear.*'"

"And you're able to see these things?"

"Lakota can see when they are blind and can hear when there is absolute silence. We possess the patience to wait for wisdom from the Great Spirit. I tell McKinley what I see and hear from the words of the Bible. They have more meaning than he knows."

I saw Amos as a complex and insightful man sandwiched between two generations and two cultures. He knew Sitting Bull and Crazy Horse, and yet there he was next to me in the bleacher, with failing eyesight, admiring his tribe's young athletes who were steeped in American culture. He knew several missionaries and government agents, and although he seemed to grasp the meaning of the Christian faith, he was beholden to many Sioux traditions.

As we waited for the game to begin, Amos told me many things about the players. Most shocking of all were the players' experiences at the Industrial School for Indians in Carlisle, Pennsylvania.

I learned that when the ballplayers were an active group of boys between the ages of ten and fourteen, a representative from the Carlisle School visited their reservation. The school masters boasted about the merits of their institution and of their star alumnus, Jim Thorpe, who had won two gold medals in the 1912 Olympics.

The school was founded by Richard Henry Pratt in 1879. Pratt, who had an interesting background as a U.S. officer, commanded a unit of Negroes known as the Buffalo Soldiers as well as native Indians who were hired as scouts for the 10th Cavalry Regiment. His experience with this unit might have given him a deeper interest in seeing the American Indian assimilate and reach financial parity with the white man—*E Pluribus Unum*: out of many, one. Pratt recognized the full Godly humanity of all men regardless of their race, which might have been his motivation for starting a boarding school with all good intentions, but after Pratt left the school, its quality diminished.

With Pratt gone from the Carlisle Industrial School of Indians, Amos was skeptical of its claims. Carlisle's original focus on academics and vocational skills had shifted to an emphasis on athletics. But the well-meaning white men from Carlisle insisted that the school would still help the Lakota children learn valuable trades like construction, clothing manufacturing, and shoe making as well as modern farming techniques. So, after much discussion with school representatives, tribal leaders were convinced that it would be a good thing for many Pine Ridge children to attend. The children would also continue their English and other academic studies while in attendance—all designed to help them assimilate.

Amos remained leery about the decision and insisted on escorting the children to Pennsylvania so that he could have a firsthand look at the school's conditions and the manner in which the children would be treated.

About twenty-five children travelled to Carlisle, some girls but mostly boys. Amos specifically mentioned two girls, Mary Yellow Flower and Bess Singing Bird, who, along with Matthew Running Bull, were the youngest ones of the group. Although Running Bull had an unusual stocky build, which was why he was given that name, all three children were small enough to squeeze into one bench-style seat on the train.

They took turns sitting next to the window and inventing games to play, but they slept most of the time. Amos sat across from them, keeping a close eye on the three youngest as well as the other Lakota children from the reservation. This was before he had lost some of his sight.

When they arrived at the school, the children were escorted to a large building called the clinic. Amos followed. The boys went into one room and the girls another.

In the boys' room, Amos saw other students from different Indian nations, along with the boys from his tribe, all standing in a long line. One by one they were checked for head lice, cuts, bruises, or other problems. The boys were stripped, bathed, and given a new uniform. It was at this point when Amos was stopped by a couple of uniformed men and was asked to wait outside.

Troubled that he couldn't stay with the boys while they were being bathed, Amos walked around the school grounds where he witnessed something disturbing. Shrouded in white sheets, the bodies of two deceased children were being carried out from an isolation ward, victims of tuberculosis.

Amos stormed back into the clinic and was met by the same men who had previously shown him the door. Running Bull saw Amos arguing with the men. It must have been a confusing and scary episode for him to witness because he yelled out, "Wise Heart," from across the room. He left the line, ran over to Amos, and tugged on his arm.

Amos was the only adult the children knew. The experience was made more difficult by the sounds of young girls crying from a nearby room. Amos began to worry for Yellow Flower and Singing Bird.

"Please don't go," Running Bull cried.

Singing Wolf, who was the oldest student from the tribe, saw Running Bull holding onto Wise Heart and dashed to their side. He tried to pull Running Bull back into the line.

"It will be okay," Singing Wolf said, trying to assure little Running Bull. "We will be fine and learn many things. Then we will be able to help our Oglala tribe grow big and powerful."

"But we're powerful now." Running Bull continued to cry.

"Yes, but we can be greater and stronger," Singing Wolf said.

Amos was not convinced. "I've seen enough here," he said to the men in uniform. "I want to take our Lakota children home."

But it was not to be. Amos was escorted back to the Carlisle Station and put on the next train to South Dakota. It was a sad day for him, leaving the care of their Lakota children in the hands of strangers.

The children stayed at the Carlisle Industrial School for four years. That was when its doors closed in 1918. The institution never quite measured up to Richard Henry Pratt's dream of a grand boarding school for Indians. But even with all of its flaws, the school's remarkable athletic program managed to turn the players into a cohesive baseball team.

From the corner of my eye, I could see that Maxwell was fascinated by my conversation with Amos, and that he had been scribbling continuously in his notebook. Now all I needed was an affirming show of talent from the players.

~ CHAPTER TEN ~

"Batter up!" Father McKinley shouted. He was the official plate umpire for the day.

The potential ballplayers on the sidelines caught my attention. There were none in uniform. In fact, there was nothing uniform about them, other than their government-issued, canvas-cloth, work trousers in varying conditions—from nearly new to nearly rags. Their shirts varied from Sunday's best to faded hand-me-downs. Some of the men had baseball shoes with or without full soles. Others had moccasins or bare feet.

While distracted by the physical needs of the village and of the Lakota team, it dawned on me that watching a few scrimmages couldn't possibly provide satisfactory intelligence on all of the men before the day was out. I needed to systematically study these athletes, and the best method would be to follow the same protocol used when I first tried out for a semiprofessional team.

I stood up and called over to Father McKinley, "One moment, please! May I have a word with you?" I looked for a way down from the bleacher. "Excuse me, please," I said, stepping between seated bottoms.

Bill Singing Wolf also came forward from right field, and as I approached home plate, McKinley extended his hand.

"I'm pleased to meet you, Mr. Gannon, and I'm sorry for not being properly introduced sooner. What can I do for you?"

"Thank you, sir. Your work here on the reservation is remarkable under such dire circumstances, and I wish to applaud your efforts along with the others from your church. But as for this game, I believe a more effective way to measure the players' skills would be to have the nine best all-around players in the field, and one-by-one have the remaining men bat a couple of rotations. Would this offend any of our spectators if we don't have a true scrimmage? They appear to desire a real game."

"Not at all," Bill replied. "The people you see here don't have anything else planned today, or tomorrow, or even the next day. We tend to live in the here and now. And if you prefer to have trials rather than a scrimmage, that will be fine."

"I'm glad to hear it," I told Bill.

I glanced around at the spectators from the reservation who were frocked in their finest, with embellishments of fringes, feathers, and beads. And although they were out to enjoy an afternoon of baseball, I realized that their manner of dress was a gesture to welcome us.

"I feel as if I'm in another world. It seems so strange to be surrounded by such an unfamiliar culture."

"I can assure you, Mr. Gannon, these villagers are just as kind and generous as any good neighbor you could hope to have," McKinley said. "So, about these nine men you'd like on the field...."

"I think I can help you," Bill said. "The men I'd like to use can stop just about anything."

"Now, that's what I'd like to see, especially after such a long trip. So, carry on, and put those good players wherever you think they'd play best."

"I guess the batting order won't matter as long as the men step to the plate in the same rotation," Bill said.

"That's right. No need for innings. We'll just tally the outs. How many pitchers do you have?"

"Three," Bill said.

"Let's rotate them in as well. Do you have a scorekeeper to track the batters' and pitchers' performances?"

"Yes. Father O'Connor has the honor." McKinley waved to the elder priest sitting on a chair behind the backstop.

I saw that he had a clipboard on his lap. We exchanged waves and smiles. "Begin whenever you're ready, then."

After I returned to my place in the stands, Mr. Maxwell was full of curiosity.

"Anything wrong?" he asked.

"No, just a slight change of plans. Who's the fellow warming up on the mound?"

"David Eagle Eye, and Matthew Running Bull is catching."

"I like Eagle Eye's form. He takes full advantage of his height to pitch. Reminds me of Duke Maner in his younger days."

The first batter came to the plate—an easy strike out. He was followed by three others, who also met the same fate, and then...

Crack.

It was a hard line drive, and what followed was startling. The short stop was airborne and vertical when he caught the ball.

"Did you see that, Maggie?"

"See what, darling?"

"That fielder stole the batter's hit. He should have had at least a single. What an astonishing out!"

"Indeed it was!" Maxwell said. "That was Andrew Running Deer. I told you that these guys were phenomenal, but wait 'til you see their best batters."

"Running Deer is very good," Amos added. "You should hire him."

"I believe I will."

As the day wore on, I felt that I had seen enough player performances to make a decision. And although the men played well, I couldn't help but wonder whether they would hold up against Major League players. The fielders were no doubt excellent, but how about the pitchers? Did the men get hits because they were good batters, or did they get hits because the pitching was not on par with top professionals?

I looked at Maggie and thought what a good sport she had been to follow along as I chased after my dreams.

"What did you decide?" she asked.

"I know these men are good. I just don't know how good they are."

"I bet you're wishing Duke were here."

"Very perceptive, my love." I sighed with a long, deep breath. "Duke's worked with so many Major League pros that he'd know instantly if these men could measure up. My gut says they're precisely that good, but my brain can't make the fine distinction. I just don't have enough baseball experience to know if they're just very good or if they're superb. That's the gamble."

"What's your biggest concern?" she asked.

"There's more than one. I've warranted to the Los Angeles League that my players will be absolutely topnotch. Furthermore, shipping a whole team to Downey, in addition to housing and feeding them, will be costly. They're not just any team—these men are Indians, and I don't know what prejudices will hamper their travels, or their stay in California. On the other hand, I can't imagine being able to put together a better team with so little time left."

"Phineas, these players are fine men. Don't worry about what others think. It's you who must worry how you think. I have my own trepidations," Maggie said. Her voice cracked, so I knew that she was about to say something that was uncomfortable for her.

"Your competitions with Mort are getting more and more expensive. I hope that you're not tapping into our nest egg just as you're about to retire."

"Don't worry, my love, we have plenty of money. Besides, this is how Mort and I sharpen our entrepreneurial skills. An unidentified failure to win against Mort could represent a failure at Gannon. But with carful analysis of my loss, I'm able to prevent Gannon Fine Meats from making the same sort of business mistake. But if I should score a win, I may be able to apply the winning strategy to the meat company."

"That's quite an interesting bit of twaddle, darling, and if it's all true, it would seem that perhaps this should be your last Gannon-Cunningham competition now that Paul is taking over the company."

"Last one? Horsefeathers! Retirement wouldn't be nearly as fun without our little rivalry." I chuckled.

But I wasn't laughing inside. Maggie's comments cut through my heart. Her concerns must have been festering for some time. I never wanted her to worry about anything and certainly not about finances. Maybe she was right about my frivolous spending. I didn't know how much longer I'd live. The economy was strong, but would it weaken tomorrow after I was gone and couldn't help Paul weather the tough times? What a wake up call! I was living life as if I expected to be a centenarian, when, in fact, my heart could give out at any moment.

With the pressure of a looming deadline, I decided that my Lakota players would have to be my entry, and after seeing their desperate living conditions, I felt that it was the right thing to do. Though unproven, the Lakota players appeared to have a fiery, winning spirit. Whereas, Mort's team would most likely consist of the very best Major League bench-warmers money could buy.

"I think I'd like to go home," I told Maggie. "Paul's had the helm long enough for a trial run. The sooner I get him up to speed as an effective boss, the better it will be for us. Do you mind if we return to Los Angeles on the next train?"

"Not at all. Since we left California, I've been a little worried for Paul, myself, wondering how his first full week as an executive was going."

Everyday I grew increasingly grateful that I married Maggie. She had been my greatest admirer, friend, and lover. I would never know whether she really wanted to stay a few more days in South Dakota or head home. That was her way. She knew I wanted to leave, and so that became her desire as well.

With score sheets in hand, and all of the players anxiously awaiting my decision on which players would make up my team, I suggested that Father McKinley, Father O'Conner, Amos, and I meet over at the schoolhouse and discuss my selections. I needed their involvement and their blessings, no matter which players were on my list.

I took Amos by the arm and helped him down from the bleacher.

"Tell me, what is it that you want to accomplish?" Amos asked as we walked across the field toward the school.

"Do you mean with these young players?"

"No, for you. I want to know a little more about you."

It was an interesting question, but one that wasn't entirely unexpected. Amos had a deep concern for the welfare of the young men, and of course, he wanted to know my motivations. But Amos seemed to have a remarkable concern for me as well. All my life I felt that I was the one who had to look after others, and here was this elderly man showing me enormous compassion that transcended our physical, racial, and cultural differences.

"Hmm," I said. "I've already accomplished quite a bit, but most immediate on my agenda, I want to retire. To do this, I must teach my nephew how to run the family business. But if you must know the reason why I want to hire a baseball team, it's so I can beat my longtime rival, Morton Cunningham. I want one final victory over my friend."

"You want to beat your friend?"

"Perhaps it's hard for you to understand and harder to explain, but we do it just for the thrill. We've been competing for years, and this game will probably be my last one against Mort."

"Is that all you'd like to achieve?"

"No, I suppose more than anything, I want to spend more time with my wife. We're planning a trip to Europe in the spring. But, actually, this trip to South Dakota has meant the world to me. I simply enjoy being with her."

Once inside the schoolhouse, McKinley beckoned us to join him in the principal's office where the four of us were seated around a large table.

"You have many exceptional players," I told the gentlemen, placing my notes before me. "And I've had a positive hunch about this team ever since I first read about them. Seeing them play only solidified those notions. But it has come to my recent attention, with regards to my sports competitions, I may have been going overboard with my free spending."

"Are you saying that you won't hire these men?" Father O'Conner asked.

"No," I replied. "That's not it at all. In fact, here are my selections: Johnny Chasing Hawk, center field; David Eagle Eye, pitcher; Luke Buffalo Warrior, left field; Pete Charging Horse, third base; Matthew Running Bull, catcher; Tom Fighting Bear, second base; Gordon Winter Cloud, first base; Andrew Running Deer, short stop; and Bill Singing Wolf, right field. Bill will also remain the team's captain."

"Those men are certainly our finest," McKinley said.

"I thought so, and you can rest assured that I will send for the players as soon as I can make the arrangements. But first, allow me to be up front with you. I want every player I hire to sign a contract. That's what players do. They sign contracts. Signed players carry a special distinction. They are considered professional. But while making a decision to hire a team, I've also made a decision to address some of my extravagant spending habits. That's why I'm only hiring nine players. If we win our first game, then I'll consider hiring more men, but that's not a promise."

"Well, Mr. Gannon," McKinley said. "I'm relieved and glad that you'll hire at least nine players." He stood up and looked out the window toward the village. As you can see by these conditions, their families can certainly use the money."

"Yes, I noticed, but before you celebrate my decision to hire a team, I want you to understand the importance of their first game. If the team loses their initial game, I will insist that they return to South Dakota immediately."

"Immediately?" O'Conner was shocked. "That's a high expectation you're placing on a first game. Even Yankee management is not that demanding on their players."

"The first game is only an exhibition to determine if we have a slot in the Los Angeles Winter Ball League. With no first win, there are no future games to play. I can't very well have a team without any baseball games, can I? So, upon losing, they will be terminated and sent packing. This may seem harsh to you, but I, too, have much riding on that initial trial."

"And if the team wins that first game?" Amos asked.

"Then they will generate enough revenue to fulfill their contractual obligations. Win or lose, by qualifying for the winter league, the gate receipts will more than cover their salaries, and surely all the other expenses which I've incurred. And, of course, the winning team always takes home more money, so there will be several opportunities for bonuses during the season."

"What do you think, Amos?" Father McKinley asked.

"I think there's a moral to this," he replied. "It pays to follow one's dream, even if the consequences are not what one expects. It is God who will ultimately decide our destinies whenever we chart a new course. Mr. Gannon followed his dream by traveling to South Dakota, and our Lakota players can do the same by going to California. If it is God's will, they will win the first game."

"I totally agree," Father O'Conner said.

McKinley nodded, too. "I guess that settles it. Mr. Gannon, I believe you have yourself a baseball team."

We shook hands to seal our agreement.

"Come," Father O'Conner said. "We'll walk you to your car."

I saw God's will for me while visiting South Dakota. It wasn't about the baseball team but about the needs of others. I was exposed to an entirely different picture of our country, abject poverty, forgotten Americans, and dedicated missionaries working hard to improve the conditions of a lost people. I felt good that I could hire my Lakota team. And though they would only earn a small stipend should we lose to Mort, it would go a long way to help them over the winter months.

I also felt quite strong during the entire trip, not needing one pill. Dr. Burton and Maggie were absolutely right—I needed a vacation. My harried life had slowed, proving there was no reason for me to push myself so hard at Gannon Fine Meats. It was time for me to sit back, put my feet up, and enjoy retirement.

~ CHAPTER ELEVEN ~

It was the fifth of October when I finally heard back from my lawyer Frank Simpson. He stopped by my office to give me the good news that he had the contracts ready for signature, and he had found an attorney in Rapid City, Oliver Scott, who would be willing to work with us.

"Mr. Scott will require a retainer," Frank explained, opening his briefcase on his lap and pulling out a small stack of papers. "Of course, the balance will be due when his work is complete. He has agreed to collect the necessary signatures on the contracts and arrange for the baseball players' transportation to Los Angeles."

"Well done, Frank. This is exciting to hear."

But it really wasn't. It had completely slipped my mind that I had told Frank Rapid City was closest in proximity to my players. I found myself in an awkward position, because I had unknowingly misled him.

I cleared my throat. "Uh, Frank," I stood up and stepped behind my chair, holding onto its back. "When I told you that Rapid City was the nearest city to my players, I didn't know about Hot Springs, which is actually much closer to them. I'm terribly sorry about the mix up, but I'm certain that the smaller community of Hot Springs was not on my globe atlas."

"Phineas, this is not good to hear. Are you saying that your players are not from Rapid City?"

"That would be correct, but the good news is that Rapid City is on the western side of the state where my players reside, and it's only a little farther from the Pine Ridge Reservation."

"The Pine Ridge Reservation? Are you telling me that your ballplayers are Indians?" Frank practically yelled.

"Yes, Frank, that's what I'm saying."

He put the papers back in his case and shut it up. "You just can't hire a bunch of Sioux—not without going through the Office of Indian Affairs in Washington, and that's going to take some time."

"How much time?"

"Weeks, maybe even a month or two. Or maybe your team won't have permission to leave the reservation until after the winter ball season ends."

"Come now, it can't take that long. It's only a rubber stamp on a document."

"It may very well be that simple, but we're dealing with Washington, and nothing in Washington D.C. is simple. A savvy businessman like you should know that."

"You're right. So what can I do with so little time to spare? The playoff game against Mort is only a month away."

"I'm sorry, Phineas." Angry, Frank stood up as if he wanted to leave. "Short of a miracle, you may have just forfeited the game."

I felt sick enough to take a pill, but I didn't want to do it in front of Frank, so I took a deep breath and continued on.

"Please sit down." I took my seat, and to my relief, so did he. "It appears as though I've sent you on a wild goose chase, and for that I must apologize. You've always been so thorough and on top of things. I'm also grateful that the contracts were prepared in a timely manner."

"Yes, they're written, but to what end? I wish you would have told me all of this sooner. Even if you had permission from Washington, Rapid City is a good distance away from the Pine Ridge Reservation. With the uncertain weather conditions in the Dakotas, your players may not see those contracts until the spring thaw. What a costly gamble! It doesn't look good for your Lakota team."

"If I listen to you, Frank, I've lost the game before the umpire's coin toss. There has to be a way to get my team here before the November game. There's a clear advantage to owning a team that has performed together for many years, and if they win a Los Angeles slot, then all the jumping through hoops will be well worth it."

"Face the facts, Phin. Time's not on your side."

"Let's go ahead and get the contracts signed as if we have the permission documents in hand, but please add that their employment is contingent upon receiving everything from Washington."

"I can do that. I've already stipulated in their contracts that they must return immediately to South Dakota if they lose the trial game. Of course, you would pay for their return transportation. But now there are other things to consider. Oliver Scott was willing to work with us when he thought you were interested in a local Rapid City team, but now I must explain that things aren't exactly as I had originally thought."

"Then send him a wire. Tell the attorney that he'll need to head out to the reservation and find those baseball players. I'll pay him for the additional time and distance. In the meantime, leave all of those Washington D.C. permission details with me."

"That—I can do."

"Good, because I want those Indians. I think they'll attract hundreds, maybe thousands more fans which will more than cover the added costs."

"Very well. It's your money, Phin. Let's just hope Mr. Scott will travel to Pine Ridge and negotiate with the Indians."

Frank picked up his briefcase and left my office. What a setback for me. I took a pill and then asked Miss Pierce to come into my office and take a letter.

"Yes, sir," she said in her proper, schoolmarm manner. She approached my desk and sat in her usual chair.

"Shall we start?"

"Yes, sir."

"This letter is to go to the head of the Office of Indian Affairs," I explained. "And I want it posted before you leave today. I don't know the addressee's name or title, so it will be up to you to discover those facts. In the meantime it's *Dear Mr. Whomever...*"

"Am I to assume you do not know the address either?" she asked.

"Yes, that would be correct. *Dear Whomever... It has come to my attention that Indians are not allowed off their reservations without the expressed written authorization from your office. As a baseball club owner, I am formally requesting...*"

"Excuse me, sir. Did I hear you correctly? Are you claiming to be a baseball club owner?"

"Yes, Miss Pierce, you did hear correctly."

"And did I also hear you say that you have a concern about Indians?"

"Yes, Miss Pierce. Now, let's continue... *I am formally requesting permission for a Lakota baseball team to leave their Pine Ridge Reservation in South Dakota immediately and travel to Los Angeles, California, so they can play in our winter league between November of this year and February 18, 1929. I will be their sole benefactor during their stay in Los Angles, providing transportation to and from the city. I will also provide their room and board while they are off the reservation. Please send to my office any necessary documents or affidavits that will grant the following men...*"

I handed Miss Pierce a list of the players' names.

"*...authorization to make this trip, et cetera, et cetera.* I should also like a second copy of the permission documents sent to the law office of Mr. Oliver Scott. You'll need to get Mr. Scott's address from Frank Simpson."

"Perhaps you'd like to explain the baseball team to me. After all, this is the first time I've heard about your acquisition."

"Not yet. I will in time."

"I understand, which means this team must have something to do with a new challenge between you and Mr. Cunningham."

"Well—if you must know, yes. I suppose that's what eighteen years—"

"Twenty years."

"Yes, of course. I stand corrected. It's quite apparent that our long professional relationship has given you mind reading skills. So, let's continue with the subject at hand. Now, where were we?"

"I believe you would like me to obtain additional information regarding names and addresses of the recipients, type a letter for signature, and post it immediately. Will there be anything else?"

"No, that will be all."

"Then let me remind you that you're having dinner tonight at the Biltmore with the Cunninghams."

"Thank you. That's one dinner that I don't want to miss."

~ CHAPTER TWELVE ~

After Jane left my office, the tightness in my chest returned. Dinner at the Biltmore with the Cunninghams was a stressful thought. I couldn't say a word to Mort about my team, especially since I didn't even know whether I'd have one. I took another pill, and while waiting for it to take effect, I began to reminisce about my father, and how he had passed away. Surely I would have a few more years left on this earth, except I was much heavier than he ever was.

The year that Gannon Fine Meats celebrated its twentieth year in business, Father bought a brand new 1916 Packard Twin-Six Touring Car, expanded the size of the slaughterhouse, and moved the corporate offices to a downtown location on Spring Street. Father also kept a slaughterhouse office because he constantly worried that our name would be sullied if we lost control of the cleanliness at the plant. It wasn't unusual for him to spend most days there, even though the slaughterhouse men were fully capable of running day-to-day operations.

Los Angeles was a rapidly growing city. Our company struggled to keep up with the demand. Should we hire more men or open another slaughterhouse? And if we did, could we continue to insure high quality meat products? Those were the questions my father and I wrestled with all the time. It was a balancing act to know how much corporate expansion was too much and how much was not enough.

Another concern was the international situation that was becoming more unstable. In the prior year, the Germans had sunk the Lusitania, killing over a hundred Americans. Newspapers predicted the United

States would soon enter into the war, so we had to ask ourselves what impact this would have on our business. At that point Father and I decided to purchase more land. Strong demand in the past required us to purchase stock from unknown cattlemen to fill the orders. That often proved to be a mistake, sometimes with unpleasant outcomes. But it did show us that we needed additional land to raise our own beef cattle in order to control quality.

By the fall of the year, we decided to drive up the coast to Ventura County where several large parcels of land were available—acreage that was suitable for two hundred or more head of cattle. We were ready to purchase one or two properties, and if the land looked promising with adequate water supplies, we were prepared to purchase more.

We couldn't have had a better day to travel. The weather was perfect, and because it was so beautiful, Mother asked to join us. I thought about asking Maggie, but she had previous commitments with her Women's Club activities. After purchasing our home on Carroll Avenue, I found myself working harder than ever to pay for our lavish Victorian. Maggie substituted loneliness with social clubs and volunteer work, further depleting time we could share together. Those were my thoughts when Father and Mother pulled up in front of our house. It seemed no matter how busy Father was, he always had time for Mother.

Mother looked lovely that day, wearing a pale gold touring suit and a wide-brimmed hat tied securely under her chin with a large, cream-colored bow. She always seemed so young for her age, with only a few gray hairs and hardly any wrinkles.

The top was down on Father's car, and the warm breeze felt good on our faces as we motored along the highway. Father and I had been working such long hours that we rarely took time to be a family, retell old stories, and just enjoy our companionship.

It took us all morning and part of the afternoon to reach the city of Ventura, stopping for lunch along the way. Once there we met the real estate broker, P.K. Morgan, or Peaky as he called himself, at his house.

Peaky's home office was easy to find and not far from the downtown district. We parked in his driveway, walked up to his front door, and rang the doorbell.

"Mr. Phineas Gannon?" he asked.

Father and I answered, "yes," and then laughed.

"Yes, we are both Phineas Gannon," Father said, "and this is my wife, Cora."

Peaky invited us inside and served us tall glasses of lemonade while we discussed our specific property needs.

"If we get started real quick like," Peaky explained, "I think we have enough time to see two and maybe three properties before the sun sets. It goes down early this time of year."

We were all eager to go. Father wanted to drive to get a feel for where we were headed. Peaky sat in the front seat with him, and Mother and I sat behind them as we left the city of Ventura and headed for the countryside.

The first property we saw was absolutely beautiful, large gently sloping hillsides of tall grass with a substantial stream that bisected the lower portion of the tract—plenty of room for a couple hundred head. There was also a wind-powered well with a gasoline-powered backup generator. On the downside, the only structure on the premises was a small, one-bedroom house that had been vacant for more than five years.

A few miles from that property, Peaky showed us a second parcel that was similar to the first, yet smaller. With more flatland for grazing, it could support more cattle.

"What do you think?" I asked Father when Peaky was out of earshot.

"Son, I think that we should talk about this after a good night's rest. Let's tell Peaky that we're driving over to Oxnard to spend the night. He can reach us at the Oxnard Hotel tomorrow after breakfast."

"A good plan," I said.

I knew my father well. He didn't want Peaky to think we were too eager to purchase both properties, though we both knew they would be perfect. By waiting a day, it would give Peaky the opportunity to discuss a lower asking price with the owner, and give Father and me time to work up some numbers. The other and most important benefit of waiting—it gave Mother, Father, and me time to be together in a relaxed atmosphere.

Although we shared most holidays together, I had forgotten how much I enjoyed the company of my parents. Mother's sense of humor and light conversation were always so pleasant, and she rightfully insisted that Father and I limit our business discussions.

Oxnard was a charming city, a few miles south of Ventura and a little more inland from the ocean. The town was famous for its large sugar factory that processed sugar from a special variety of beets. The center of town had a beautiful hotel that was recently renovated after a devastating fire. For that reason, Mother wanted to stay in Oxnard. She liked the fact that the Oxnard Hotel was new and fresh, not to mention the largest hotel between Los Angeles and San Francisco.

That night at dinner, and after I had a chance to bathe, Father and I went over our numbers, calculating what sort of return we could expect on these properties and what would be the most we could afford.

"Son, didn't you find it odd that the only house on either property had been vacant for over five years?"

"Yes, I did, and I regret not asking Peaky about that."

"It could be a cause for concern. But even if there were a good explanation, it will take some money to fix it up. All of which ought to be factored into our offer."

"I agree, but I'm also pleased that there is a house," I said. "We'll need caretakers for those ranches, and that house, as poor condition as it's in, may have to be home to a couple of hands while it's being repaired."

"And let's not forget that both properties will need equipment and additional outbuildings."

Mother interrupted our conversation with her usual charm. "How about continuing this business talk after dinner over coffee? Right now I'd like to enjoy the company of my two favorite men."

"You're right, dear," Father agreed, smiling at Mother.

While seated at the dining table in the hotel, looking at my parents, I was distracted by loving thoughts, wondering how the years could have whizzed by so fast. Father and Mother were getting on in age, and spending more time with them meant more than they would ever know.

The following morning, I joined my parents for breakfast in the hotel dining room. We hadn't heard from Peaky, but then, we didn't expect him to call on us until later. In the meantime, Father and I decided on the amounts we would offer for the properties, along with the terms and conditions, however, Mother had other ideas.

"Let's visit the seashore before seeing Peaky," she suggested to the two of us as we were finishing our meal. "We can have lunch at some ocean view restaurant. Really, you two, I'm having so much fun that I don't want the day to end."

"You're right, Mother. Let's stretch the day out as long as we can."

"Okay," Father concurred. "We can meet Peaky later. I'll let the desk clerk know that we'll see him at his place after lunch. From there, we'll head home as soon as we cinch the deal."

We packed our things and loaded the Packard. Mother was once again wearing her pale gold touring outfit and her wide-brimmed hat. It was another beautiful day, so we left the top down on the automobile. There we were merrily off on another adventure, singing "Down by the Old Mill Stream" in perfect three-part harmony, heading for the ocean.

I sat behind Father and sang tenor, Mother sang soprano, and Father had the bass. We sounded so good, we sang it again. Perhaps it was the singing that distracted Father momentarily, which is why he didn't notice the farm truck heading toward us as he turned left at an intersection.

I didn't know how he could have missed seeing it. It seemed as large as a whale, full of sugar beets on its way to the factory. With a full load it would have been impossible for the truck driver to stop in time, but he slammed on his brakes.

It was like watching every thing in slow motion. I saw the truck skidding toward our Packard on Mother's side with hundreds of sugar beets flying over the truck's cab about to pummel our automobile.

Upon impact, Father and I were thrown from the car. We both rolled down a small embankment. He landed not far from me.

"Are you okay, son?" he asked as he tried to get up.

I could see that he was dazed and suffered a substantial cut on his face. We were both badly bruised, but aside from that, we were okay. Then in an instant it struck me.

"Mother!" I yelled.

"I ran back to the car. Father hobbled behind. All we could see was a corner of Mother's pale gold outfit buried under the front of the truck, along with mangled parts of the Packard covered with mounds of sugar beets.

Father was paralyzed by guilt. He knew that it was his inattention that caused Mother's untimely death. I wrapped my arms around him and listened to his shouts and cries that would forever ring in my ears. What I remembered most about this sudden tragedy was how it made me cling much tighter, love more strongly, and feel more deeply.

One of the officers at the accident site drove us back to the Oxnard Hotel, and at the suggestion of the desk clerk, I called for a doctor to give Father a sedative and tend to his wounded face. Perhaps I needed a sedative as well, but there were too many things to deal with at the time.

I called Peaky and cancelled our afternoon appointment without explanation. I couldn't describe to anyone what I had just experienced, but I had to call Maggie and tell her there had been an accident, that Mother was dead.

Maggie was shaken as well, but she remained strong enough to come up with a plan.

"I'll call Morton and ask him to drive up to Oxnard and get you. He can help you make arrangements regarding Mother. He's the friend you need right now."

"You're right, Maggie. Call him and let him know where we are."

Father was never the same after that day. He died the following year of a sudden heart attack.

After visiting Doc Burton and experiencing regular intervals of tightness in my chest, it was hard not to think of my own mortality.

I heard Jane knock on my office door. The vial of pills was still in my hand, so I quickly slipped it into my pocket.

"Yes, Miss Pierce, come in."

"Mr. Gannon, I have that letter ready for you to sign."

"What letter?"

"The letter to the Office of Indian Affairs. If you would please sign right here, I can post it on my way home."

"Oh, yes, of course. Good work. Let's get this sent off right away."

~ Chapter Thirteen ~

When the Biltmore Hotel opened in 1923, it was the largest hotel west of Chicago, and perhaps the most luxurious. Rich marble columns and opulent chandeliers enhanced its striking architecture. Stars like Mary Pickford, Harold Lloyd, and Buster Keaton were sometimes seen dining at one of their exclusive tables.

Morton was already seated when Maggie and I entered the ballroom, where the orchestra was playing soft dinner music. I felt out of sorts in my tuxedo, but my wife was absolutely stunning in her new lilac gown.

"Phineas dear," Maggie spoke in her sweet muted voice. "Please don't get too wound up tonight. I know you're excited about this baseball match, but really, this is not a business dinner for two men. There are four of us here tonight wanting to have fun, dine, and perhaps enjoy a dance or two."

"Don't worry, darling. I won't say much about our baseball game. The pleasure comes from saying as little as possible about the players and our strategies, leaving both us wondering about the other's team. It's all in good fun. We'll save the details for game day. I can't wait to see Mort's face then."

"Because he'll notice that your team is actually a tribe?"

"But it's much more than that. Now, remember, not a word more to either Mort or Jeanne about my team. All I want from Mort tonight is a sense of what he thinks of his players. He'll place a wager with me, and the size of his bet will let me know how he values his team.

That is, unless he's bluffing.'"

"You and Mort are just like children."

"Don't worry, my love. Mort and I will keep our baseball talk to a minimum."

The maitre d' walked up to us. "Mr. and Mrs. Gannon, I'll show you to your table now."

Maggie curled her arm inside mine, and as we neared the Cunningham table, Mort spotted us and rose. "Good evening, Maggie, Phin."

"Hello, Mort," Maggie replied.

"You look so elegant, my dear," he said before a brief kiss on her cheek. "Phin, I don't think you deserve such a lovely wife."

"Believe me, I don't. Where's Jeanne?"

"Oh, she'll be right back. She's powdering her nose or something."

"Then perhaps you two gentlemen will excuse me," Maggie said. "I think I'll let her know that we're here."

"Splendid idea!" Mort said.

"And I promise, dear, that Mort and I will hush up about sports by the time you ladies return."

"If that's true, then I can't wait to tell Jeanne."

Maggie headed toward the ladies' lounge, and I waited until she was out of sight before leaning slightly toward Mort.

"I hear that you've managed to hire some men from the American League. Any names that you care to share?"

"Not on your life," Mort snapped back. "I'm more interested in putting a little money on the game, aren't you?"

"A little money? Ha! So, you haven't much confidence in your Major Leaguers. Duke told me you paid handsomely for them."

"And Duke is correct, because I want winners and not some two-bit minor team from where? Kansas? Nebraska?"

"The Midwest. I'll give you that much."

"Ooo, I like that—where it gets too cold and too dark before the regular season ends. They can't be that good. Sounds like I've got the upper hand. Tell me more about your ballplayers."

"Unlike your Major League *washouts*, they're a strong-looking lot who have played together for years. I bet they'll outperform your men, which you've merely thrown together, giving me the greater advantage over your last-minute scratch team."

"Are you willing to bet heavy on that—let's say one hundred dollars?"

"A hundred dollars!"

"Come, come, Phineas, certainly you have that much confidence in your team."

"Of course, I do," I snapped back. "But a mere hundred dollars? Make it five hundred, and we have a bet."

I probably should have just doubled the bet, but Mort was now four hundred dollars ahead in our ongoing tally. I needed the higher wager to take the lead, and besides, Mort's shocked expression was priceless. I thought he would gag on a five hundred dollar bet, while I felt as if I were betting the farm. Win or lose, I could certainly afford five hundred dollars.

"Okay, five it is!"

Mort stuck out his hand to shake on it, and as I sat there foolishly laughing at the whole thing while Mort scooted closer to me.

"Phineas," he said in a lowered voice. "There's something I've been wanting to confide. It's not sports related, it's personal."

"Oh?"

"I have a mistress, a young and gorgeous movie starlet. Her name is Virginia, but I call her Ginny."

"Mort! Why would you do a thing like that?" I looked at his weathered face and nearly bald head.

"Ah, don't be so shocked. All of my friends at the club have sexual liaisons on the side."

He looked at me as if I were some fool for not lusting after someone half my age.

"I purchased a small Hollywood bungalow, so I can have a few late night trysts. It's a pleasant arrangement. I give Ginny cash for the rent. She deposits it into her bank account and then mails the money to my accountant in the form of a personal check. It makes my real estate investment appear sound because the rent is substantial, and it's always on time."

Mort was laughing, almost crying as he choked on his chortling, but I found his humor distasteful. I couldn't fathom any part of the situation as funny.

"My accountant hasn't a clue. He believes Virginia is an eighty-year-old widow living in that bungalow of mine." Mort continued to laugh. "And that's the way I like it."

"But why risk your marriage over some tart?"

"It keeps me feeling young, invigorated. I couldn't begin to tell you what it's done for me."

"I can. It's ruined your reputation."

"Not in my circles—you're the lone exception. Last spring I traveled to a Chicago trade fair with Ginny. It was great fun. I even managed to get some business matters resolved along the way. We met up with an Illinois congressman who was also with his lady friend. I tell you, Phineas, it's more normal than you know."

I was devastated. My longtime friend was gambling with his community standing, his marriage, and maybe his position with Silver Suds Soap.

"How long has this been going on?" I asked.

"About a year."

"I've heard enough. You must break this off immediately. Jeanne's happiness is far too important to Maggie and me. We are her dear friends. How can I look at her tonight and not feel tremendous dismay? Morton, you've put me in an awkward position. I can't imagine what your eighty-year-old father would say if he were to find out. Silver Suds reputation of purity will be permanently tarnished, and all because of your torrid affair."

"Calm down, Phin. I didn't expect this sort of reaction from you of all people. We've been friends nearly our entire lives."

"I am reacting as a friend should. Don't you understand that your immoral actions are fodder for the tabloids? You're always fishing for free publicity, but a headline that ties you with a Hollywood Jezebel can't be good for Silver Suds."

"No one is going to run to the newspapers with this information."

I was so furious that I began to sweat. I dabbed my forehead with a table napkin. "That's where you're wrong. This town is full of snitches for cash. Movie magazines, newspaper columnists, extortionists—they all know how to profit from scandal. They may not be able to recognize you, but they certainly know the likes of every new starlet who comes to town. And don't think for a second they won't put a gumshoe on you so some housewife in a beauty parlor can read all about Virginia's dark side. I want you to do the right thing and stop this philandering at once. I detest this awkward position you've placed me in with Jeanne. Remember your wife Jeanne? She's Maggie's good friend, and she's my friend, as well."

I sensed that Mort had some remorse, but not over his affair. He only regretted telling me about the matter.

"You don't have to scold me. Just don't act surprised if you should happen to see me out with a beautiful, curvaceous brunette."

"Fine, I won't scold you. And I won't act surprised, but I'll not cover for you."

"That's fair. Now, smile, Phineas. The ladies are returning."

~ Chapter Fourteen ~

Ten more days had passed, and with no communication yet established between the Rapid City attorney and my Indians, I decided to invite Duke over to my house. I thought we could discuss backup plans over dinner, assuming any reasonable options existed. He was well aware of my predicament, so before we met, he had called all of his Major League contacts to find out which ballplayers in both the American and National Leagues had not signed for winter ball.

Good old Duke Maner, a superb ballplayer who had turned down a chance to play with the Brooklyn Dodgers in the late 1890s. Back then he was known as the speedball king by many catchers and pitchers. He pitched to me on several occasions when we played semipro, so I knew what the term "speedball" truly meant.

I first met Duke when I tried out for a position on a Pasadena team. I was only twenty. Duke was playing for one of the best Los Angles teams and was hired by Pasadena just for the day to pitch to all the prospective players. The manager of the Pasadena team figured that if a batter could get a hit off of Maner, then he would be good enough to sign. I struck out the first round of hitting, but before I returned for rounds two and three, Duke gave me some valuable tips regarding my swing. When I returned to the plate, I got a hit and was signed.

I loved playing baseball, but I was only a one-year wonder. Couldn't get my average above .200 in my second year and was subsequently dropped from the league.

Outside of Hollywood circles, Duke was one of the biggest celebrities around Los Angeles. Dignitaries usually invited him to ballgames. The mayor, senators, congressmen, state and local legislators—they all wanted to be seated next to him. Duke always made a game more exciting because he could spew facts and background color better than any other person around. And being seated next to him often guaranteed a positive newspaper photo for any politician.

After working all day at the courthouse, Duke finally stopped by my house. Even at his age, a big, tall, strong-looking man like Duke made the perfect bailiff. Most assuredly his connections helped him land the position. It was good employment for any retired ballplayer. He claimed that the job was only difficult when witnesses or the accused got out of hand, but most of the time he was entertained by listening to interesting cases.

"It's no use, Phin," Duke said as we sat in my parlor waiting for dinner to be served. "There simply are no more available players in the Majors. The best we can do is to find out which local semipros haven't signed for winter ball and work from that list—but here's the problem with that idea. Any ballplayers we hire at this late date won't play well enough to beat Mort's team, nor will they meet the standards of the Los Angeles Winter Ball League."

"I like Vernon's team, and Santa Ana has several good players. What do you think of hiring one of those teams outright?"

Duke laughed. "Those men aren't available. Around the middle of July they begin to look for winter ball work."

"Can we offer them more money?"

"Absolutely not. If any of them reneges on a deal, especially at this late date, they become poison, blackballed for years by every club around. Family men are dependent on year-round play and would never put their careers at risk. No, Phin, I'd say we're in a tough spot. We need those Indians more than you know. We're also cutting this much too close, which means I won't have any coaching time with the men before the first game."

"How about a good minor league team in the Northeast or Midwest?"

"Not a chance. Their regular season ends before ours, so they've already left for winter ball."

I took a deep breath and sunk down deep into my overstuffed chair. I hated it when Mort got the best of me.

"Have you heard of any big names on Mort's team?"

"No, no names. Mort would keep that information close to his chest, but I know he's made several inquiries in search of players. I believe he's snagged a few more Major Leaguers to play with his local men."

That was upsetting news. Whenever I got uptight about this sort of thing, I'd smoke a cigar, which was not an easy thing to do at home. "There are too many variables and risks, and with no contract signatures gathered, I suspect my South Dakota lawyer could be snowed in. We also need to keep in mind that it takes a few days to transport the players before the game."

"Are you thinking of conceding the Los Angeles League slot?"

"Are you kidding me? Why, that's the last thing on earth I'd do! Solving the player problem is what makes the competition so interesting, and this baseball idea is the best battle I've ever had with Mort. But then, if all else fails, I will, with great regret, concede to Mort without a single game played. Devastating! It would be absolutely devastating."

I stood up, excused myself to check on dinner, and then returned.

"Come on," I beckoned Duke as I headed for the front door. "Let's go for a walk. Our cook seems to think it will be another half hour."

Duke, always the health-conscious athlete, was eager to go, and I was anxious for a cigar. We stepped outside, and after we were out of sight, I puffed a large cloud.

"Ah…I feel much better now. Maggie despises these things."

"They're not good for you."

"Of course they are. They help me think. It's ballplayers like you who shouldn't smoke them. I'm a meat executive who needs a good cigar to recognize my day-to-day battles, visualize solutions, and tackle the difficult challenges. I love being an entrepreneur. It stimulates my mind, and a good cigar is part of every businessman's regimen."

We continued walking down the street. Both of us in deep thought.

"I wish we had an alternate plan," Duke said, breaking the silence. "The way it appears—we're stuck, and I don't know what else to do. Does that cigar-stimulated mind of yours have something to suggest?"

"No, not yet. Maybe I should switch brands." I chuckled, but only to mask my fears as we continued on our walk. "I'm thinking this competition against Mort will probably be my last. Don't think my heart could stand another, and death would be the only thing standing in my way of a rematch."

"I'm sad to hear that," Duke said. "I guess it means this baseball game is even more important than anyone could know. What would you like me to do?"

"Just move forward as if the Lakota players were on their way here, and as if they were the very best team we could muster. Think positive thoughts about them. That's all we can do. Let's not have any regrets or any thoughts that they are not a fully capable team. Now, how about uniforms? Will they be ready?"

"I've purchased plenty," Duke insisted, "and in different shirt sizes to err on the safe side. The pants are all cinched below the knee, so the length won't be a factor. And let's face it—they're all ballplayers, so there can't be much variation in their sizes."

I looked at my watch and decided it was time to turn around. Duke followed my lead, and we headed back to the house.

"While visiting the reservation, I noticed our Indians had no uniforms. That means they'll need everything. I'd even include undergarments. That Oglala tribe had dire needs, so don't leave anything to chance. What about the equipment?"

"It's not a problem to round all that up. The catcher's gear, too. I have many resources. As far as I can see, all we need are your Indians."

"You know, Duke. Even though it's quite nerve rattling, I rather enjoy all of this raw excitement. Everything necessary to bring my Lakotas to Los Angeles is in place. And now it depends on everyone doing their part to make it happen on time."

~ Chapter Fifteen ~

With game day rapidly approaching, I began to believe that I'd have to forfeit, but then Frank telephoned me at my house.

"Oliver Scott's Rapid City office received the contracts," he told me, "and the money for the team's rail passage."

"Finally! But is that the only good news?" I asked, clenching my candlestick phone and its receiver in my hands.

"If you're asking whether Mr. Scott has taken the contracts to Pine Ridge, the answer is, I don't know. His secretary could only say that Mr. Scott's office was in possession of the package which I had sent."

"Doesn't that attorney know we have a deadline?"

"Yes, Phin, he knows. But even if he had the signed contracts in hand, the players can't step off the reservation without permission from the United States government."

"I hope Scott isn't waiting for those D.C. bureaucrats before getting my players signed. It's not necessary because of the contingency clause," I reminded Frank.

"That is correct."

"Well, then, what's the hold up?" I hated it whenever I became so angry that I was tempted to display outward signs of wrath, but I kept my composure. It also helped that Maggie happened to walk by while I was on the telephone, though I suspected she had been in earshot of my voice.

"I'm not sure," Frank said. "I'll call his office today. But I must tell you, your long distance calls are expensive and more numerous than

I thought we'd need. Every call requires that I pay a person to wait on the line, oftentimes over an hour, while the long distance operator connects our calls."

"At this point, whatever it costs. Just get those Lakota players here before the game. That should tell you how much I'm willing to spend on this team."

"Has there been any word from the Office of Indian Affairs?" Frank asked.

"Not a peep," I replied, and then buried my face in my left palm for a moment. "I found out yesterday that Mort has his full roster. The league president told me when he telephoned to ask if mine was full as well. I told him, yes, but I had transportation issues to work out. Frank, I don't enjoy thinking Mort has skunked me, but that's the way it's beginning to look."

I paced as much as the phone cord allowed—a mere five feet.

"Honestly, Phin, why must you add all of this extra pressure to your life? Isn't your company stressful enough? I suppose I will never understand what pleasure you and Mort derive from your competitions."

"They're fun. Work is—well, it's work. There's a huge difference, you know. The only thing that's stressful with our competitions is the unknown, so please see what you can find out."

As I said goodbye, I began to feel a little nauseated. My hands trembled so much that I had difficulty hanging up the receiver. Frank was probably right. I might have been adding too much pressure to my life. I reached for my bottle of pills, and to my great relief, there was one dose left. Dr. Burton had said he wanted to see me in a month, an appointment which I had no intention of keeping if it weren't for the empty prescription bottle. I grabbed my hat and car keys and headed for Downey.

Although Donald was pleased to see me for a follow-up examination, he wasn't happy that I had swallowed every pill that he had dispensed. His dismay over my rapid consumption of medicine was somewhat tempered by my slight weight loss—eight pounds.

As he took his time listening to my heart, I could tell by the look on his face that it wasn't good news.

"You're pushing yourself too hard," he said. "Take some time off, an extended vacation, and not just a short hop to—"

"Hot Springs, South Dakota."

"Well, wherever it was, your time away wasn't long enough. You need to slow down and relax much more."

"I'll have lots of time off come next spring."

"Oh?" Donald sat on his stool and began writing on my chart.

"I'm retiring. My nephew Paul is taking over the reins."

"I hope you last that long. Even though your weight is improving, I'm worried about the number of pills you're taking. What's going on? Is this management change causing you that much stress?"

"No, it's something else."

Donald peered over his glasses, casting his wide eyes of concern upon me. I could always depend on his silent scolds. A couple of times he stood behind me in the buffet line at the country club, closely monitoring how much I was piling on my plate. I dutifully returned the extra portions.

"Doc, I'm involved in one of the most exciting things I've done in years."

"With your business?"

"No, it's nothing to do with the company, but it has the potential to be profitable. Remember on my last visit here I took an article from your *Holbrook's Magazine*?"

"Vaguely. Why?"

"It was about a talented Lakota baseball team in South Dakota."

"Don't tell me you and Mort couldn't wait at least a year between…"

"That's right. We're at it again. You know as well as I, my ticker won't last much longer, and surely you don't expect me to sit around and wait for an undertaker to show up at my front door."

"Nor do I want you to hurry him along," Donald choked slightly on his words.

I felt a twinge of sorrow for my doctor friend. As much and as often as he had to face inevitable realities with his patients, many of whom he had known for years, end of life discussions were never easy for him.

"I had a feeling you were going for one more competition."

I smiled. "Of course. Mort's ahead by $400. I can't die when I'm that far behind. Ah, Doc, you'll love our rematch. We're entering competing teams in a baseball playoff to see who will garner the last slot in the Los Angeles Winter Ball League."

"And some of these Lakota players are on your team?"

"No, the Lakota men *are* my team—the whole team." For a moment I caught myself dreaming of victory, until Donald interrupted my gratifying thoughts.

"That's just about the craziest thing I've ever heard. Why on earth would you hire men from South Dakota when right here in Southern California we have some of the finest baseball players in the country?"

"Availability is a big problem, and that could be an issue for Mort. But my Lakota men are great athletes. Wouldn't you pay a little extra to see a team of Indians play against National and American League pros?"

"I suppose I would."

"There, you see. That's what I'm counting on—people want to see the unusual, and they're willing to pay a little extra for the opportunity."

"Does Maggie know about all of this?" Donald handed me my clothes, and I began to dress.

"You mean, does she know about the Indians? Absolutely. She was with me in South Dakota when I hired them. Miss Pierce, Duke Maner, and a couple of attorneys also know, but we're the only ones. Mort's clueless, and that's the way I like it."

I pulled up my pants and tucked in my shirt. "I know the baseball idea is risky and fraught with frustrations, but it's also tremendous fun. On the other hand, to Maggie's delight and yours, too, I may be forced to forfeit my crazy Indian fantasy if this competition doesn't start going my way."

"Forfeit your fantasy? Ha! That will be the day. Phin, I've known you for a long time, and I could never imagine you giving Mort an easy win, even to spare your body the added stress."

"It wouldn't be deliberate. My concession would only occur if I couldn't get my team here in time for the game. And if I can't, I lose—a forfeit, a stinking, ugly, forfeit. Now, that's real stress on the heart."

I always suspected that Donald vicariously enjoyed my gamesmanship with Mort, so it didn't surprise me that he asked, "So, what's the problem?"

"Regulatory nonsense—the usual Washington, D.C., paperwork. All I need is permission from the Office of Indian Affairs to get my players off the reservation. How would any ordinary citizen like me know this? It's a problem, Doc, a huge problem. Some low-level bureaucrat in Washington, D.C., has my letter of request sitting in a pile on his desk while I'm popping these pills like candy, trying to stay calm until my baseball players get permission to leave South Dakota. I detest the thought of losing to Mort without a single game being played. That's not an honorable defeat, and it keeps me up nights."

"Hmm…Phineas, I'm thinking that the Office of Indian Affairs is under the Department of the Interior, and if it is, perhaps I can help you."

"Honestly?"

Donald left the exam room and returned with his personal address book. "I went to school with Hubert Work," he said, turning its pages. "We both graduated from the University of Pennsylvania Medical School. He still writes me on occasion."

"And just who is this man?"

"The Secretary of Interior, that's who he is."

"You mean, I just might be back in the running?"

"Maybe."

"Maybe is good, and certainly better than an outright loss to Mort." I started to laugh. What a miracle pulled out of thin air! "Can I call Secretary Work? Or, better yet, can he contact my attorney in South Dakota?"

"Calm down, Phineas. You'd better let me handle this. Have your secretary send me the details, and I'll see what I can do."

"That's the best medicine you could ever give me! This game between Mort and me must be part of a divine decree."

"I'm not making any promises, but since Hubert and I are good friends, it gives me an opening to at least ask if he'll help you out. But promise me, after this competition you're taking a long vacation."

"Absolutely, my friend."

I walked out of Dr. Burton's office a happier man with a fresh bottle of pills and a new outlook. Life was sweet, and I was still a contender!

While in Downey, I decided to stop by and see Karl and Ruth. I needed to let them know there could be some people staying at the ranch using the bunkhouse, possibly for an extended stay. The question that came to mind was whether to tell my caretakers the guests were Indians, though not just any Indians. They were educated Lakota and sophisticated enough to play America's favorite pastime.

I thought about it a little more. Karl loved baseball, and so he would calmly handle the news and be amused by my ballplayers' celebrity, but I had my doubts about Ruth. This might make her a little testy—or possibly extremely testy. After all, ten guests, though only for ninety days, was quite a bit to ask of anyone, so I decided to postpone telling my caretakers about the Indians until I knew they were actually coming.

Ruth was standing at the back door when I parked my Cadillac behind the ranch house, and Karl was nowhere in sight.

"Hello, Ruth. How are you today?"

"Fine. What brings you out this way?" she asked.

"Just a routine doctor's visit. I decided to stop by while in town. Is Karl around?"

"He's in the barn. Let me ring him up."

Ruth gave a few short tugs on the rope that rang the farm bell, calling Karl to the house. We watched him poke his head out the barn door. He took off his hat and waved it.

"Afternoon," he yelled, walking toward the house.

The barn was about a hundred yards away and slightly downhill. In the meantime, Ruth invited me inside for a glass of iced tea.

"Karl will be a while. He changes his coveralls and shoes on the back porch before coming inside."

I sat at the kitchen table and watched Ruth chip a large piece of ice off of the block in the ice chest and place it into a pitcher of tea. It reminded me of her fastidious nature. She was such an organized and skilled housekeeper, it seemed like it was no bother for her to quickly make a cool drink. The ranch house was always immaculate, and her vegetable and flower gardens were always beautifully maintained and enjoyable to walk though. Even the henhouse she tended was clean and well kept.

"Are you all right?" Ruth asked.

"Yes, yes, I'm fine."

While she was talking, I may have been in a fog, wondering how much I should tell my caretakers. I tried to visualize Ruth's reaction to the Lakota players, and it wasn't good.

"Are you sure you're okay? Ruth asked again.

As Karl entered the kitchen, wearing his clean overalls, I quickly wiped my distant appearance from my face.

"Well, Phin, what brings you out this way?" he asked.

"I had a routine visit at Dr. Burton's."

"You're okay, I hope."

"Oh, yes, I'm fine, but I felt that I should talk to you about the bunkhouse. Monday after the party, I had the occasion to go inside and see what state it was in."

"Were you unhappy about something?" Karl asked.

"No, not at all. In fact, I was delighted to see that it was in quite satisfactory condition, which made me think that perhaps the bunkhouse could be put to good use on occasion."

"And just what did you have in mind?" Ruth spoke up.

I sensed a twinge of suspicion in her voice, so I chose my words carefully.

"When was the last time that bunkhouse was used—a year ago, maybe two?" I asked.

"At least that long," Ruth answered.

"I thought maybe the bunk rolls should be untied and given a good beating. Allow them to air a bit. The place also needs a thorough sweeping and the cob webs removed. You know, in case for some unknown reason we might have the need to put a group of people up for the night or longer."

"That sounds reasonable to me," Karl said.

"How many people did you have in mind?" Ruth asked with a

strong air of skepticism in her voice.

"Ah, Ruthie," Karl said to her. "He said it was a *just in case* situation. Didn't you say that, Phin?"

"Let me just say that nothing is absolutely certain right now." I sipped my tea.

"You see, Ruth, nothing's certain" Karl added. "So how would he know how many people?"

"I just thought it would be a good idea to always have the bunkhouse ready in case a need should ever arise on short notice."

"How short of notice?" Ruth asked.

"Now look here, Ruth." Once again Karl came to my rescue. "There's no way he'd know all of this. Let's just clean the place up and see what happens."

"Thank you, Karl, and you, too, Ruth."

That was all I wanted to say, and I was relieved to make my exit with everyone smiling. Without knowing all the facts, there was no reason to upset Ruth with additional details.

While driving back to Los Angeles, I thought about what I had said to our caretakers. I didn't really tell them anything untrue. At this point, my Lakota team was technically hypothetical—at least it was until I had signed contracts from all of my players and written permission from the government.

It did seem like fate was smiling upon me. Who would have ever thought that Dr. Burton had the magic connection with the Secretary of the Interior?

~ Chapter Sixteen ~

"Maggie, darling, the postman is here," I said, watching him climb the front steps of our home, two at a time.

My wife liked to greet the gentleman whenever he delivered our mail. It was one of those things a husband discovered when semi-retired. She thought I didn't notice the twinkle in her eyes every time she stepped out onto the porch to meet him. The charming young man was young enough to be Maggie's son, but what was most amusing was how Maggie acted appalled whenever I teased her about it.

As I watched Maggie through the window chatting up the postman, I laughed to myself. I felt sorry for the chap. He had to make his rounds within a certain time frame, and yet he politely talked to all the ladies up and down Carroll Avenue.

Since Paul took over most of the day-to-day business at Gannon, it felt odd not dashing off to the office first thing in the morning. My nephew, who didn't have a drop of Gannon blood in him, seemed to embrace his new position at the family business. I didn't dare go into the office any more than necessary, so the employees would see him as the authority figure. I also wanted him to grow in confidence. With my future hanging in the balance, it was reassuring to have someone competent to replace me. I couldn't imagine what I'd do if he were an imbecile.

Ah, the carefree life of a retired husband. My biggest concern at the moment was my competition with Mort, but everything was out of my hands. All I could do was to wait.

"There's a letter for you from Washington," Maggie said, returning indoors. "It looks official." She handed me the mail and then politely reminded me, "Don't forget, we're having the Johnsons over for dinner tonight. Paul's coming, as well."

"I suppose that means the Johnsons' daughter Mary will be here, too."

"Of course. Claudia and I think they're well suited for each other." Maggie gave me one of her alluring smiles. "And you know perfectly well it's a good way to encourage a relationship."

"Yes, yes, I do remember. Perhaps helping our timid nephew with his love life would be a minor payback for all of his good work at the company."

I reached for my letter opener on a side table and sat down in my favorite chair. Finally, I thought. This could be my moment of truth. The delays, though minor, had been agonizing. My hands shook as I worked the opener under the envelope's flap. Maybe the doctor was right. Maybe I was getting too old for these competitions with Mort.

After I unfolded the letter, I briefly skimmed it. "Aha!" It was exactly what I wanted. The positive response and accompanying documentation from Secretary Work's office bolstered my sense of victory. The Interior Secretary made a personal visit to the Office of Indian Affairs and cleared the way for my Lakota team. A second copy of the authorization was sent to Oliver Scott's office in Rapid City, but I still didn't have the signed contracts, and there was barely enough time to transport the men to California in time for the game.

In the thrill of the moment, I jumped out of my chair, wasting not a second. I couldn't help but do a little dance all the way to the hall. I picked up the telephone and called my attorney.

"Frank, it's here! The permission letter is in my hand as we speak, and it shows that a copy was sent to Mr. Scott in Rapid City. My Indians are free to travel to Los Angeles. Isn't that wonderful news!"

"Yes, Phineas, it is good news. I had heard from Mr. Scott just moments ago. He called from his Hot Springs Hotel, another expense

I might add. He mentioned that his office is also in receipt of the letter, and that all of the contracts are signed and ready to mail back to my office. The only thing left to do is purchase the train tickets, but apparently there is a question about that."

"What sort of question? What's the holdup?"

"Apparently the team wishes to add another man, and without that additional person, they don't want to leave the reservation. Therefore, Mr. Scott will need more money wired to him to purchase a tenth train ticket."

"Oh, for crying out loud!" I sat down on a hall chair. "That Rapid City attorney is sure pushing my deadline. Very well, wire him more money if that will keep those players happy, but do stress to Mr. Scott that I'm only paying salaries for nine players. Those Indians can jolly well divvy up their money for that tenth player. This team has already cost me a small fortune, all unrecoverable expenses unless they win that first game against Mort."

"I'll relay that message."

"No, wait. I'll pay the salary for the tenth guy, and I'll wire Mr. Scott the money for the tenth ticket. Their tribe needs the money, and it will make Duke happy if I have at least one bench warmer. Just make sure Scott knows that I'm not authorizing any more players to come, and I'm not changing my mind with regards to the Los Angles League. If they don't win that playoff game, they'll be spending the rest of the cold, nasty winter in South Dakota. There's no way I can justify the cost of this team with any other league."

"I understand."

"So, where do we stand, Frank?" By this time my palm was sweating so much I had to wrap a handkerchief around the phone to hold it. "Will Mr. Scott be able to get my Indians on a train in time for our game? We're cutting this awfully close."

"He's fully aware of the time constraints and has assured me that if we can settle this one issue of the additional man, then he'll promptly proceed."

"Great Caesar's ghost! If this attorney doesn't make our deadlines, I'm sending him my pharmacy bill."

After Frank and I hung up, I looked at the desk calendar by the telephone and realized that from now on everything must fall into place like clockwork, or my Lakota players would not arrive in time to challenge Mort's team.

I swallowed another pill, and after my chest pains subsided, I felt that maybe I was a little too harsh with Frank.

~ Chapter Seventeen ~

"Please help yourself to more mashed potatoes, Paul," Maggie said at our dinner table.

"Thank you. Don't mind if I do."

"Here." I handed Paul the gravy boat. "This will put a little more meat on your bones. I'm a bona fide authority on that," I said, laughing.

"Really now, Phineas." Maggie gave me the eye. She despised that sort of table talk.

I was a bit crude in front of Maggie and our other women guests. "Sorry, ladies, I apologize. It was an unfortunate slip of the tongue. We gentlemen joke so often that we sometimes forget the delicate nature of our women."

I was doubly sorry because I knew that Paul wanted to make a good impression on Mary, and there I was blurting out such nonsense. Mary seemed like such a wonderful match for Paul—beautiful, intelligent, and very sweet. Paul graciously gave me an opportunity to show that I wasn't such a big blubbering idiot.

"Tell us, Uncle Phin," Paul said, "how did you know that your big Long Beach beef giveaway wouldn't harm the financial health of the company?" Paul looked at everyone around the table and told the story. "For eight hours Uncle Phin gave away a free pound of beef to hundreds of people in Long Beach, and he did it out of sincere compassion. His Long Beach customers were going broke trying to take care of a dying child, but after Uncle Phin's brilliant marketing idea, their butcher shop flourished. You must have calculated the financial loss to your company prior to placing the advertisement, and it must have been substantial."

"That's quite perceptive of you, Paul, but it was only two steers."

"But two steers is a lot of beef," Mr. Johnson said.

"Only for one day," I said. "I knew Gannon Fine Meats could quickly recover. Father and I had done it before, though under a completely different circumstance. We wanted to help this dear young couple, and we knew we could do it."

I didn't like to talk about my good deeds with others, but if the truth were known, Father and I had a deep desire to help those in need. Years earlier we donated ten head. At that time, we felt a hard financial pinch from our gift, but eventually we worked through it.

By 1906, Gannon Fine Meats had been in business for ten years. Our financial reserves were slim because we had reinvested so much back into the company. And although we were certainly capable of withstanding the ebbs and flows of the market, the company was too young to weather major problems like cattle epidemics, sharp regulatory shifts, or untenable tax hikes. All of which could have wiped us out or severely hurt us, but as odd as it seemed, charity never adversely affected our bottom line.

It was early morning in April of 1906. Maggie and I were still in bed when I noticed a strange look on her face.

"Did you feel that?" she asked.

"Feel what?"

"A tiny tremble. Look." She pointed to the teardrop crystals hanging from a nearby lamp. "They're moving slightly, but not enough to make a noise."

"It's nothing to worry about," I assured her.

Later that morning, we heard the devastating news. San Francisco was hit hard. We could only imagine the size of the earthquake, because hundreds of miles away, other residents in Los Angeles had felt it, too.

About a week later, when the full scope of the catastrophe began to sink in, Father and I wondered what we could do to help. There were thousands of homeless people, all in need of sustenance. We knew a few cattlemen from the Sacramento area, and together we pooled our resources and pledged almost fifty head for the relief effort.

Father sent me to Sacramento on the train with the ten head to insure the stock would be a true donation to the needy. With so many scam artists around posing as legitimate charities, our fellow cattlemen were happy that I could spearhead the endeavor and make sure our livestock was given to a trustworthy agency.

The government's relief program was coordinated from Sacramento, where I had arrived twelve days after the quake. I made arrangements to stay with a fellow cattleman whose ranch was not far from the capital. He was kind enough to keep the Gannon cattle fed while I sought the best way to distribute the beef.

I decided to travel to San Francisco to see its current conditions. There was much confusion due to the size of the disaster, so it seemed prudent to personally assess food delivery systems. My goal was to leave Sacramento in the morning and return late that night, but to my surprise, getting to San Francisco was much easier than leaving. I rode the train to Oakland, and upon arrival around noon, I discovered that the return train was completely sold out. People had no permanent place to go, so they opted to leave the area—mostly by train. I would have to wait another day for transportation back to Sacramento.

Thousands remained homeless, and while walking the streets of Oakland, I saw large tent cities that had sprung up in many areas.

Within my first hour, a young woman stopped me and asked, "Do you have some water for my child? She's so thirsty."

The woman needed more than water. She looked exhausted and dazed. I wasn't sure this mother would be able to hold her child much longer. She was also carrying an oversized carpetbag while the little girl straddled her right hip.

"I'm not familiar with Oakland, but I'll do what I can to help.

Where's your husband?" I asked.

"I don't know. We were separated early this morning when we stepped off the ferry. I've been looking for him ever since."

I thought the woman was about to faint, so I said, "Here, why don't you let me carry your bag and daughter?"

She was grateful for my offer. Together we walked in search of a water fountain, stopping everyone along the way for directions.

Not only did we soon find a place with water, but we also found a line of people waiting for a free meal. It was the Salvation Army's tent.

"Have you and your daughter eaten today?" I asked.

"No," the young woman replied.

"Then you should get in line and have a hot meal. Surely your husband will eventually pass by this facility."

The Salvation Army appeared to have an organized method of meeting the needs of the people, and when I noticed they were serving free beef stew, I was convinced that this was where the ranchers' donation should go.

"May I speak with someone in charge?" I asked a Chinese volunteer, a middle-aged woman, who was dishing out large scoops to hungry patrons. "I'd like to make a large donation of fresh beef."

She handed me the serving ladle and her apron.

"Here, take over. I know who you need, but I'll have to find him first."

For the next hour I served countless hungry people as they passed by my station. I even noticed the young woman with the child had been reunited with her husband. It was a wonderful free service the Salvation Army was providing. And when the large kettle of stew had almost run out, someone stopped by, replacing it with a fresh batch, allowing me to continue serving without a break.

I finally met with the person in charge and made arrangements to have the cattle shipped and butchered for their relief program. But for the rest of the day and into the night, I continued serving meals until

6:00 a.m. That was when I caught the train to Sacramento, and from there, a second train back to Los Angeles.

I knew better than allowing my mind to wander while entertaining guests for dinner, but the good will gesture Father and I had executed at a time of dire need was so gratifying. I often think about him and how much we enjoyed building a business together and sharing our good fortunes with others. There were many more things I wanted to do with him, but like Mother, he died too soon.

I looked across the dining table at Maggie and couldn't help but wonder how many opportunities she had missed because of all the races I had invented with Mort. I realized my race against time was now more crucial. How much more joy could I squeeze out this life? How much more love and knowledge could I impart before my last goodbye?

"Shall we retire to the parlor for coffee and dessert?" Maggie asked.

I glanced at all the guests around the dinner table and then looked at my wife. "Yes, dear, let's do that."

~ CHAPTER EIGHTEEN ~

At last, word had come, but with no time to spare. Frank stopped by my house to personally deliver the good news. My Indians had boarded the train in Hot Springs and were headed for Los Angeles. My spirit overflowed with delight. The players would arrive on Friday evening, a day and a half before our big game on Sunday. If they made all of their connections, I'd be in the playoff. On the other hand, if something should go awry with their travels, I would be out everything and Morton's team would have the winter ball slot.

With this knowledge, I drove out to the ranch. I needed to tell Ruth and Karl that they should expect my Lakota ballplayers on Friday evening, and if my men won on Sunday, they would be guests until February. As I motored toward Downey, I prayed that my disclosure would not be confrontational. I knew I should have said something sooner to my caretakers. Although my delay was prompted by a lack of information from all parties concerned, I regretted my earlier decision not to fully divulge my plans.

When I pulled into the drive that led up to the ranch house, I noticed two young children playing on the front lawn. The older one was splashing water from the fountain. How odd, I thought. Karl and Ruth had children, but they were grown, and I didn't recall anything about grandchildren.

As I parked my car in its usual place behind the house, I noticed another oddity—Thelma Albright was hanging several diapers on the clothesline. Her two infant twins were sleeping nearby on a blanket, shaded by an umbrella.

"Hello, Mr. Gannon!" Thelma shouted over the clothesline as she continued to hang laundry.

"Good morning, Mrs. Albright."

Thelma's husband David, a good customer of mine from Whittier, owned a successful but modest butcher shop. So why were his wife and eight children staying at my ranch?

As soon as I walked in the back door, I saw Ruth kneading bread dough on the kitchen table.

"Hello, Ruth. What's going on around here? I just saw Mrs. Albright and a few of her children."

"Don't worry, it's not permanent, only until the first week of January. It was Paul's idea."

"Paul?"

"Yes. He's a fine young man, and what a big heart he has. He reminds me of you, always thinking kindly toward people in need. I must tell you, Phin, it was a good thing you had Karl and me clean up the old bunkhouse. We got it spic-and-span just in the nick of time."

"I'm glad to hear that," I said, while thinking of the terrible housing jam I was in.

"We have all of the kids staying in the bunkhouse, except the babies. They're sleeping with Mr. and Mrs. Albright in the guest bedroom. Oh, and by the way, the food bill this week was unusually large, so you might get a call from the grocer authorizing more credit."

"I see. That's fine. Uh, where is my nephew?"

"Why, I suppose he's at your downtown office," Ruth said.

"Of course, I'm sure he's there. I haven't been going into work much these days, now that Paul's been running things."

"And Mr. Albright says he's been doing a splendid job."

"Yes, I can vouch for that."

My mind was spinning out of control. I couldn't stop thinking about the terrible mess I was in. The circumstances were somewhat dire. I had no place to put ten players, and I had no idea if any of the hotels had available space or would accommodate Indians. But even if I could find a hotel or boarding house, the additional expense would cut deep into my baseball profits.

"Will you excuse me, Ruth? I must be running along."

I didn't dare say anything, nor did I ask Ruth anymore questions. If Paul made this decision, I wasn't going to discredit him in front of my caretaker, but on the other hand, I couldn't get out of the house, back into my car, and down the highway fast enough, thinking about what on earth possessed Paul to invite this large family to stay at my ranch. I would soon find out once I reached my office.

~ Chapter Ninteen ~

I was too frustrated and furious to enter Paul's office, so as I walked past Miss Pierce's desk, I asked her to send him into mine.

"Yes, Uncle Phin?" Paul said as he entered and sat down in front of my desk.

"Paul, it's come to my attention that you have invited the Albright family to live at the ranch. Do you want to explain this?"

"Sure." He beamed with pride. For some odd reason, Paul was almost giddy as he began his story.

"I was on my way to Whittier last Sunday to call on Miss Johnson. As you know, I'm sort of sweet on her these days, and I sense the feeling is mutual."

"That's nice to hear."

"I'm so glad you think so, Uncle Phin. She's a nice girl. I was to escort Mary to church that morning but realized when I was about halfway to Whittier, I was much too early, and so I stopped in at the ranch to kill a little time."

"And were the Albrights staying at the ranch when you were there killing time?"

"Oh, no, not then, but I did have a nice chat with Karl over coffee. He explained to me that the bunkhouse had been thoroughly cleaned, and it was ready for any *just-in-case* situation, should one happen to arise. He said it was your idea."

"Yes, I'm afraid it was."

"I left the ranch and continued on to Whittier, arriving at the Johnsons' house on time, but after I parked in their driveway, I smelled smoke. At first I didn't see any signs of a fire on the horizon, but the odor kept getting stronger and stronger. Mr. and Mrs. Johnson and their daughter Mary must have smelled it too, because they all stepped outside, onto their front porch. About this time we could see the first plume of smoke about three blocks away, followed by a large flame. Then all of a sudden we heard fire trucks ringing their bells."

"'Where do you suppose the fire is?' Mr. Johnson asked."

"I told him I'd find out and report back." I got in my car and drove in the direction of the fire. Then, to my dismay, I discovered that it was the house of one of our best meat customers, Mr. Albright."

The Albrights had eight children. The oldest, a daughter fifteen, and the two youngest, twin boys five months. That morning, Thelma had prepared breakfast for everyone while her husband was shaving, and their oldest daughter was dressing the young ones for church.

Thelma had been up most of the night with fussy twins, and was, most likely, too tired to fix breakfast, but there she was in the kitchen preparing a morning meal. As a consequence, when she left the kitchen momentarily, she didn't notice that the dish towel, which she had been using to check on her muffins, was left too close to the stove. The towel caught fire and fell into a box of old newspapers—the papers that the Albrights used to start their stove fires. By the time Thelma returned to the kitchen, the blaze was too big for her to handle, so she got everyone out of the house. Mr. Albright was in his trousers and undershirt, with shaving soap over half of his face. But everyone else was fully dressed for church. In only a few minutes, the house was engulfed with flames, and a short time later, completely destroyed down to its foundation.

During the church service, the preacher announced that the congregation would collect donations of furniture, clothing, and household items. Mr. Albright felt he could afford to rent another house after the first of the year, because the holiday months were generally good for meat sales, but for the next few weeks they would need some temporary shelter. Many people offered a spare bedroom, but no one was able to offer enough space so this large family could stay together until then.

"I tell you, Uncle Phin, I sat there squirming in the pew, listening to the minister's plea for additional help while looking at the outstretched arms of Jesus in the stained glass window above the altar. Then, all of a sudden, I jumped to my feet and offered the bunkhouse at the ranch. It was the Holy Ghost and your generosity that inspired me to help this family."

"I always claimed that you were a quick study."

"The next thing I heard was all of these *amens* echoing around the sanctuary. The joy of giving was exactly as you had described to me."

"Good work, Paul."

What else could I say? I was glad for my nephew and proud of him, and yet, as I sat there listening to him, I felt the weight of the world on my shoulders. With a bent elbow on my desk, I rested my head in the palm of my hand.

As wonderful as his goodwill gesture was, all of his philanthropy was overshadowed by the question at hand: *Where on earth am I going to put my Indians?* Mindful of many racial prejudices, the ranch was probably the only place they could stay, but what was I going to do with the Albrights? My Indians were on the train and heading for Los Angeles, and I had less than forty-eight hours to move the Albrights out of my bunkhouse. What was I going to do?

I knew that I shouldn't fret about it. I even thought that I should go home, spend a pleasant evening with Maggie, and then with deep prayer and meditation ask God for an answer. But actually, I knew better. There were doers in life, and there were spectators. In my youth I had questioned God. Why would He always give me some of the most burdensome problems to solve? Was it some sort of heavenly prank? But in time, I discovered that it was not a prank but a true divine honor. I had come to the understanding that God had created certain people on earth to resolve difficult situations like housing the Albrights. And, over time, I had come to realize that I, too, was dependent on the talents of others for all the products and services which I was incapable of providing. We all had a role to play using our God-given talents. Problem solving was mine, and I was ready to meet this one head on.

I stood up from behind my desk and shook Paul's hand. "That's all I wanted to know. Now, grab your hat. We're going to Whittier. We have a mountain to move and not much time to move it."

Paul was undoubtedly confused, but I promised to share with him the entire story before the day was over.

~ CHAPTER TWENTY ~

As far as my nephew was concerned, any excuse to go to Whittier where Mary Johnson lived was a good idea, and the fact that he could drive my Cadillac made it all the more exciting. I doubted that we had the time to call on Miss Mary, but one never knew.

Though he was a reasonably successful butcher, Mr. Albright was never able to own a house as long as new babies kept coming. And as far as I knew, he was always on time with his rent. He certainly was never behind on his meat bills.

"Paul, I need to know why Mr. Albright can't rent another place any sooner than the first week in January."

"I believe it's because he's short of funds."

"That goes without saying. Any family who loses everything in a house fire is bound to be short of funds. What I want to know is why a landlord can't help this family by allowing them to move in sooner, collecting their initial rental payments over time. They're a decent family. David is an honorable businessman, and so help me, I'm going to get to the bottom of this."

The Albrights had so many children that there was only one other rental house in Whittier large enough to house them. Unfortunately, its owner, the same man who owned the house that burned, was not willing to budge on the rent. He even escalated the lease amount after learning what caused the fire.

Paul knew where the landlord lived, so he drove straight to his house.

"You go inside and find out all that you can," I said to Paul. "It will be good for you. Do a little negotiating. I'm going to wait in the car and take a pill."

"A pill? Uncle Phin, since when are you taking pills?"

"Since little things like this started getting on my nerves. Now, don't tarry. Go inside, work out some deal with the landlord."

As I waited for Paul, I noticed a "for sale" sign on a nearby house. Though the place was much too small, it did give me an idea. Maybe instead of renting another place, the Albrights should consider buying.

The thought of purchasing property conjured up other sad memories of the time when my parents and I set out to buy additional ranch land. Shortly after Father died, I drove back to P.K. Morgan's house in Ventura to find out whether the two parcels were available. Peaky said that one of them was indeed sold, but the other remained for sale. The owner had even dropped the price considerably. It was the property with the small house.

I remembered how much Father and I thought it was worth at that time and how much our company could afford. Remarkably, the owner's new price was much below the original asking price, so I made an offer and bought the land.

A few months later, an adjacent property owner approached me and asked if I wanted some more acreage, so I bought his land as well. The total amount for both was much less than the original two parcels, and with two contiguous properties, it was a much better management situation and financially a much better deal. Father would have been so pleased. I visualized him smiling down from heaven when the two properties became mine. Rather than feeling anger toward God or others over the tragic accident, I felt my Heavenly Father's love and providence as circumstances I couldn't imagine led to a favorable outcome. The painful passage through my darkest hours strengthened my resolve to overcome future challenges and heartbreaks, offering me hope for a better future.

Paul returned to the car with the news that the landlord had changed his mind. Renting a second house to the Albrights was completely out of the question—almost completely. If the Albrights would agree to a higher rent—an obscene amount—he said he'd reconsider.

"I think the landlord thought I'd foot the bill," Paul said. "But he was wrong."

"Good work. I have another idea. Do you see that 'for sale' sign on that bungalow over there?"

"I see it, but you can't possibly believe that all of the Albrights could fit in that tiny house. It's probably only a two-bedroom place."

"Yes, but on that sign is the broker's name and address. Let's see what else he has for sale."

Paul and I drove a few blocks to the broker's house and discovered that he did have a couple of larger homes available.

"Would you like to see them?" the broker asked.

"Yes, but not right away," I replied. "Paul and I need Mr. Albright. He's over at the butcher shop, and he'll want to see these houses as well."

When we arrived at Albright's Butcher Shop, David was extremely busy. Not only was this his best season for meat sales, but many local residents, knowing his plight, decided they could help by simply buying a little more meat at his store. And though David's shop was full of customers, his eldest son and number one assistant convinced us that he could handle things for a couple hours.

We drove to both available houses, following behind the real estate agent along the way. The larger of the two seemed to be perfect for the Albrights. It was outside the town limits, making its location not quite as desirable, but its nice yard and more affordable price were quite appealing. More important, it could be financed for about the same amount as rent payments. David only lacked the down payment, and that was where I could help.

The next stop was Homer Johnson's bank. It was after hours, but Homer was very pleased to accommodate us. I could either agree to cosign for the loan until the bank was comfortable with the equity in the house, or provide the down payment. I chose the latter. I knew that David was the sort of man who would repay the money in due time. His honor and sense of self-worth would prevent him from taking charity. On the other hand, if he couldn't repay his debt to me, it would be fine. The down payment, which I was happy to provide, wouldn't put a dent in my bank account, and where else could I find a better place to invest money but in the happiness and welfare of others?

Before Paul and I left Whittier, David had closed the deal on his new house and had a modest loan which he could afford. The church and the community now had a place to take the donated furniture and other various household items, and once again, I was moving forward with my baseball endeavor. My Indians might have motivated me to quickly find a house for this homeless family, but that was the way the Lord worked in my life. Whenever I set goals and pushed to accomplish them in an efficient and timely manner, oftentimes there were Godly barriers hindering an immediate success. But those divine detours along the heavenly highway gave me a chance to be a blessing to others. The Albrights just happened to be one of those divine detours.

"I hope you're not sore that I housed the Albrights at your ranch," Paul said as we motored back to Los Angeles.

"Not in the least! And just because you're one heck of an executive, I'm buying you dinner."

Paul's generous spirit gave me the grandest compliment. I loved my nephew, his big heart and concern for others made me confident that he was the best man to take over the company. Paul had been with me since 1918 when the flu epidemic hit our Los Angeles area with a vengeance. The state had either closed or threatened to close down many public places, even the beaches.

Fortunately, Ventura was not as affected, which meant that my new ranch hands were able to keep our slaughterhouse supplied. But with Father gone and Ruth and Karl bedridden with the disease, I was running the company from my Spring Street office and tending the cattle at the Downey ranch. What made matters worse, two of the men at my slaughterhouse had succumbed to the disease, adding more responsibilities to my ever-increasing list of duties. I vowed to their widows I'd keep paying their spouses' wages for the remainder of the year, though the added slaughterhouse duties further increased my workload.

Jane took over many of my downtown tasks, while Maggie nursed Karl and Ruth at the ranch. With two very sick people there, we had to quarantine the place. It meant that Maggie had to cook, clean, and tend the large garden as well. She was tough during those dark days, and not the least bit afraid of the flu. I often wondered if she didn't frighten the germs away with her bold determination to get though it.

There was one bright spot in all of this. Paul wrote us from Chicago. He was only fourteen but wanted to come to California and help. He was an answer to prayer. Though inexperienced and with little weight on his bones back then, he managed to keep up with some of my best men at the slaughterhouse. It was Paul who made it possible for me to keep my promise to the widows of my deceased employees. His work ethic demonstrated great promise.

If you were young and wanted to be seen with the local avant-garde crowd, the powerful, or any number of Hollywood stars, then the *Musso and Frank Grill* was your destination. It was located in the heart of Hollywood not too far from Paul's home. I thought it would be a treat for him. And since I wanted the owners to be one of our Gannon customers, I was happy to patronize the place.

"Table for two?" the maitre d' asked.

"Yes, please," I replied.

We were quickly seated, and after we placed our orders Paul ducked his head slightly.

"Uncle Phin," he said softly, "don't turn around, but across the room and over your right shoulder is Mort. At least it sure looks like him."

"Oh?" My immediate reaction was to turn around, and, yes, it was Mort, and he was not with Jeanne. He was sitting across from his mistress, Ginny. I quickly turned back and faced Paul. "Just ignore Mort. I think they're about to leave, and it would be best if we allow them to go without our acknowledgement."

Paul was visibly startled. "It doesn't look like they're leaving. He's holding her hand."

"Please don't stare. I shouldn't say anything, except Morton recently told me that he was having an affair. I had managed to put it out of my mind, that is, until now."

"I bet you've been ruing this moment, hoping that you'd never run into them.

"Well, of course."

"She sure wears a lot of lip rouge."

"I saw that, too. What's more, she's about the same age as Mort's two sons, who are graduating from Harvard soon. I tell you, sitting here upsets me terribly."

"Should we leave?" Paul asked.

"No, I think if we leave now it would create a far more embarrassing situation for all of us. Let's order and pretend we saw nothing. We can talk about something else."

"Like what?

"Like my new baseball club."

"You have a club?"

"I might as well tell you, now that this seems to be the moment for revealing secrets. I do have a baseball club, but only if all of my players arrive in Los Angeles before Sunday. They're from South Dakota. Maggie and I saw them play while we were out of town. You should invite Mary to the game Sunday afternoon."

"I'd love to, but I can't. I'm having dinner with her family. Things are serious between us. I want Mary to be my wife, but I think it would be too soon to say anything to her or to Mr. Johnson until Christmas. After all, we just met two months ago at your party. Even December seems a little forward, but I know she's the right one."

"I knew instantly that your Aunt Maggie was the woman of my dreams, but knowing that you've found the right partner is only a small fraction of the marriage equation. You must believe that you're mature enough for a lifetime of commitment and that you have the fortitude to stay the course when the waters are the roughest. Those are the greatest parts of this decision."

"Mr. Cunningham apparently didn't take this advice."

"There we go again, talking about Mort. I don't wish to cast aspersions on my dear friend. I have my own foibles, but I can say with a clear conscience that infidelity isn't one of them. To break the bonds of marriage is symbolic of breaking our bond with God. It is a Holy Sacrament, and I hope that you consider this fact before you ask for Mary's hand."

"Rest assured, Uncle Phin, I've given it much thought." Paul paused briefly as he looked over my shoulder toward the front door. "You can stop worrying about Mort and his lady friend. They just left."

I drew a deep breath.

~ CHAPTER TWENTY-ONE ~

It was after eight o'clock when I arrived home. Maggie was sitting in the parlor next to the window, reading a book when I walked in the front door.

"Is that enough light for you?" I asked, kissing her on the cheek, and turning on a second lamp. Her sweet perfume left a pleasant, lingering fragrance.

"I suppose not, but when I started, the sun was streaming over my shoulder. I was so wrapped up in this story that I didn't notice how dim the light had become."

Maggie closed her book, stood up, and gave me a hug. It was a long embrace, and as we held each other close, she instinctively knew that something was not right in my life.

"What happened today, darling?" she asked. "Is there something serious on your mind?"

I chuckled. "Something serious is always on my mind."

"Then it was only a silly notion of mine. I sensed that you had a terrible day."

"No, actually, Paul and I had quite a remarkable one. We found a house for the Albrights, a Whittier family that was left homeless after a fire."

"I heard from Ruth this afternoon. I guess she didn't know about the new house then."

"She and Karl both know now. The Albrights have a lovely home just outside of Whittier yet close to David's butcher shop. It needs a little work but nothing significant."

"I'm glad to hear that." Maggie helped me remove my jacket. "And I'm relieved that your day wasn't troubling. When I first looked up at you, it appeared as if you had lost your best friend."

"No, I didn't lose anyone. I'm just a little tired. That's all."

Maggie always amazed me. She knew that I was distraught. I wanted to tell her everything about Mort because we never kept secrets. But I would never betray my friend. What good would it do? Anger Maggie? Cause pain to Jeanne? No, I decided early on not to mention anything to Maggie about Mort's lascivious affair.

"Let me draw you a bath," Maggie said. "The help has left for the day, so it will be quiet and relaxing for you. I can tell you have much on your mind, and the warm water will make you feel much better."

"Thank you, my dear. I would much appreciate that."

As we walked up the stairs holding hands, I realized that this small demonstration of intimacy had been neglected too often over the years. It now pained me to realize that I had sacrificed significant time with my wife to assure a good income for us. But to what end? Those valuable, lost moments could never be recaptured.

As I disrobed, I heard water running in the bathroom next to our suite. Maggie knew exactly how high the waterline should be so that my gargantuan body didn't overflow our oversized tub. If I had taken better care of myself, perhaps I wouldn't have needed a custom designed tub.

I stepped into the tub and sunk deep into the water.

"Lean back," she said sweetly, placing a folded towel under my head. Maggie pulled our small bathroom stool next to the tub and sat down. "Just relax, darling."

She filled her sponge from the tub and drizzled warm water over my exposed shoulders. The pampering soothed my skin down to the core of my being. I felt complete. Ah...I didn't realize how much I needed this. Her soft hands massaged my neck and scalp. I closed my eyes as she gently rubbed my temples.

"You make me feel so contented and most of all, loved," I told her.

"Keep your eyes closed, darling," she whispered in my ear.

I heard her stand up and walk across the room. I peeked. She was holding a new box of Morton's soap—his deluxe *Sterling Pure* line. There's nothing sterling or pure about that man, so using his soap wouldn't make me feel clean.

"Not fair. Keep your eyes closed while I bathe you from head to toe."

I waited in great anticipation. I wanted to open my eyes, but imagining what would happen next was more wonderful. If I should live only one more day, I would want to spend it with Maggie and with all the affection of this evening.

"Lie still, darling. I won't be long," she said.

I continued keeping my eyes closed, imagining tender, sensual moments with my wife in the soft glow of the bathroom lights. But my thoughts were abruptly interrupted by Maggie's struggles to open the box of soap.

"Can I help you with that, darling?" I asked.

"No, I can get it," she replied. "Maybe I should say something to Morton about his packaging."

I watched her biting the edge of the box.

"Excuse me. I'm going to get a scissor."

"Or maybe a knife would be better!" I shouted as she scurried out the door and down the hall.

Morton Cunningham was the last name I wanted to hear. Both he and his floozy ruined my dinner with Paul, and now his overwrapped bar of soap was about to ruin even more.

Except—I knew Maggie would return, and we would have a blissful night.

~ CHAPTER TWENTY-TWO ~

Friday Evening

Bright oranges and yellows filled the western skies over Los Angeles, and a few tones of purple rounded out the splendid evening horizon. The dazzling sunset reminded Duke and me that the mild seventy degree temperature would soon fall sharply once the sun was completely out of sight. From our park bench in front of the railroad station, we listened to the sounds of street cars and automobiles while watching a Hollywood filmmaker call it a wrap after shooting all afternoon against the city backdrop. Numerous couples were out for a Friday evening stroll, and shopkeepers, who had posters in their windows, hoped the pedestrians would be lured inside on the only night they had evening hours.

"The train's a half hour late," Duke said, closing the cover of his gold watch. He slipped it into the pocket of his cardigan. "But don't start worrying. It's usually not on time."

"Shall we go inside?" I asked. "No sense waiting out here in the dark until we know more about this train."

As we stood, our bones cracked slightly. We had lost our youthful prowess, although Duke managed to hang onto a pitching position at the annual Old Timers Game—a couple of innings was all his arm could handle. Yet, even though our glory days of baseball had passed, our competitive spirits were stronger than ever.

Duke had always dreamed of managing a winning team in the Los Angeles Winter Ball League, and I was happy to give him that chance. Mort, on the other hand, was forced to open his wallet wide and hire a retired coach from the Boston Red Sox, which he felt was worth every dollar spent. I always loved the excitement of business, its deal making and the risk taking. Mort was undoubtedly a superb businessman, but I had the keener sense of baseball. I had to laugh— my long time friend Mort thinks he knows the baseball business. He was only a spectator and never a player.

"Duke." I smiled, unable to contain my exuberance as we strolled back to the station. "I'm going to rib Mort good on Sunday!"

"Well, I wouldn't poke too much fun at him. Mort managed to sign five men from the Majors—three from the American League and two from the National. And I can assure you, he paid handsomely for them."

I wrinkled my face. "Second-string stragglers are what those men represent. Mort's real strength is in his local talent, and they can't carry him. But if our Indians qualify on Sunday, they'll be a fabulous act."

I gestured large with my hands and arms, much like a circus ringmaster. "The Los Angeles Lakotas! What a headliner, a great curiosity that will surely bring out the fullest crowds on Sunday afternoons." I placed my left hand on Duke's shoulder. "I tell you, they'll be front office gold, and all the other teams will be eager to play our Indians."

"Perhaps initially, but once we get into the season they won't appear so unique."

"Oh, Duke! Even if our men lose now and then, the Los Angeles purse will provide a handsome return."

"Let's keep our focus on beating Mort's team, because if we lose, you'll be sending our first-rate players back to South Dakota without any purse or headline benefit."

I lit a cigar and puffed a large cloud. "That's the financial risk I'm willing to take."

"And quite a big one. Let's see, you have all their transportation costs, their meals and lodging, plus you had to buy uniforms and equipment, and that doesn't count all the time and expense you incurred with Frank Simpson and that South Dakota attorney. Oh… and how much was that bet you have with Mort?"

I shrugged my shoulders, displaying full confidence that my decisions were brilliant, though deep inside I wondered if I were spending some of Maggie's retirement fund. I opened the large door to the terminal building for my friend. "After you."

We looked up at the arrival board and noticed we had to wait another twenty minutes, but that didn't bother me. It would only trouble me if my men weren't on the train. Then what would I do? I wished I hadn't had that thought. The anxiety was starting to tax my heart.

"I think I need a pill," I told Duke, but instead I opted to sit quietly on one of the waiting area benches.

"It is a little nerve-racking," Duke said. "Even I'm feeling a little tense about the whole thing."

Duke noticed the evening edition being delivered to the terminal's newsstand. "Stay here while I buy a paper," he said.

Duke loved keeping up with the daily news, and I was curious to know if the paper had announced our game. He returned, thumbing through several pages, until he pointed to a specific advertisement in the sports section.

"Get a load of this, Phin. There's a half page ad here for our game on Sunday. That was nice of the Los Angeles League to announce it."

"Believe me, that's Mort's work. He's an incurable publicity addict. Look how difficult it is to read that ad with all of those soap boxes on display."

"It says, *Another fine Cunningham-Gannon Competition.*"

"Aha! Cunningham is mentioned before Gannon, which means it's absolutely Mort's work. And look. My Gannon Fine Meats logo is way down in the corner."

Duke continued to read, *"Sunday at 2:00, Morton Cunningham's superb Major League players will challenge Phineas Gannon's highly acclaimed Midwestern team at Fiesta Park.* The ad also names the teams, *the Los Angles Silver Suds vs. the Los Angeles Lakotas.* I thought you weren't going to tell him about the Indians."

"I didn't, but I had to give the league our team's official name. They just don't realize our players are real Lakota."

"I suppose the name doesn't reveal much. After all, Cleveland has the Indians."

"Is that all there is in the ad?" I asked.

"No, there's more. Mort declares here that everyone who buys a ticket to the game gets a free bar of soap—but, as you and I know, his soap giveaways are normal."

"That's my friend Mort."

Reading the newspaper did help ease my nerves, and when the train finally arrived, Duke and I strode out to the platform and watched the conductor step off one of its cars.

In the glow of the dim station lights, we saw the first Indian standing in the doorway. It was Amos, wearing a loose-fitting, deerskin jacket that had intricate beading sewn on the back and fringes that dangled from its sleeves. He was also wearing deerskin pants and black, western-style boots.

"Ha!" Duke quickly dammed up his laugh. "Well, Phin, it looks like you've hired a senior citizen team. That Indian's nothing but an *old timer*—a *real* old timer. What is he, seventy? Eighty? A hundred years old?"

"That's not amusing, Duke."

"No, it's not. And if he's one of the players, you can certainly count me out as your manager."

"Don't just stand there. Let's at least go over and greet the gentleman."

Slowly and deliberately Amos managed the first step, but it took both Duke's and my assistance in order for him to navigate his last two steps onto the platform.

"You're obviously one of our Lakotas," Duke said, greeting the elderly Sioux.

"Amos Wise Heart," he replied. "But you may call me Amos."

"Glad to meet you, Amos. I'm Duke Maner, and I assume you already know Phineas Gannon."

"Yes, my friend Phin," Amos said. "It is a comfort to see a familiar face."

"We're so glad to see you, Amos. *Aren't we,* Duke?"

"Why, yes." Duke had difficulty wiping a grin from his face. He wore that look now and then when he wanted to poke fun at me.

I was glad to see Amos, but where were the remaining men? I reached inside my coat pocket for my vial and removed the cork stopper. Amos seemed quite interested in the blue medicine bottle and moved to within inches to watch me swallow one of its tiny pills. I didn't know what to make of his curiosity, but it seemed rather odd— an old man standing uncomfortably close, watching me take my pill.

"You have deep troubles," Amos said to me.

"Troubles, you ask?"

"No, I don't ask. I tell you," he replied. "You have many concerns from the past and many concerns in the future."

I didn't wish to comment on such a personal concern. Besides, before the pill had a chance to reach any degree of effectiveness, an enormous sense of relief came over me as the young, muscular players stepped off the train. I could tell that Duke was quite impressed. They were prime examples of Sioux athletes, big and strong, and all dressed in Levi pants, western-style shirts, and like Amos, government issued boots. On their heads were cowboy hats that had either one or two eagle feathers tucked into their hat bands, and the emblem of the medicine wheel was stitched on the front above the brim. Most of the men also had a small chain of beads hanging from their belts.

Whew! My game with Mort was officially on, with one day to spare. Though we wanted more time to work with the men before the game, at this point, I was thrilled to have a team, any team, for Sunday's competition. But something was bothering Duke. He pulled me away from the players and spoke in a confidential tone.

"Phin, there are only nine players here, plus that old man. You promised me a full roster for the season!"

"Calm down. You only need nine players on Sunday. When Oliver Scott said he needed more money for another Lakota, I wrongly assumed it would be for another player."

"Well, it's not. It's that old guy Amos."

"But he seems to comfort the team, so perhaps paying for Amos to join the players wasn't such a bad idea."

"No, Phineas, it was a terrible idea. I need some backup guys—at the very least twelve men."

"After we win the playoff, you'll have all the backup men you'll need."

"And where will we find these players? You know perfectly well that the best men are already signed."

"Duke, baseball is a sport, but it's also a business. Why should I pay for the transportation of all those extra Indians when after tomorrow's game Mort will sell me all the extra players we'll need. He *will* lose, and I'll be there making an offer for his best players. His Major Leaguers will want to stay in Los Angeles where the best money is."

Amos moved in close to see our faces. It was obvious that he wanted to size up Duke. And then he did a strange thing. He began to talk to himself in his native language. Duke and I didn't quite know what to make of it, so we just assumed it was some Lakota ritual or some sort of prayer. Bill Singing Wolf, who was also standing nearby, came to our rescue and pulled Amos aside, keeping him occupied until he finished his Lakota chant.

I noticed that the players appeared apprehensive and unsure what to do in this foreign land, but Amos, who also had bouts of arthritis and some hearing deficiencies, was not the least bit affected by the newness of the situation. Seemingly dependent on his sixth sense and unwilling to allow his maladies to hinder his duties as a patriarch, he lifted his fully extended right arm and ordered the men to follow him.

"This way," he commanded as he shuffled his feet a couple of steps in the wrong direction.

"Sorry, sir." Duke politely touched Amos on the shoulder. "I believe you meant this other way."

"Yes, you are correct," Amos agreed and turned about-face. "This is the way," he firmly commanded again.

Once inside the station, I couldn't help but notice the spectacle the Indians had created. Whispers and prolonged stares by passersby abounded. All of this curiosity merely demonstrated to me the remarkable potential of my team.

I pulled Duke aside. "These Lakota look terrific, don't they? And look how much interest there seems to be in our players!"

"I see. Now let's hope the Los Angeles League will be as satisfied with their baseball skills."

"Duke, I can feel it in my bones. They're going to be great! When we get to the ranch, have them try on their uniforms. I don't want last minute problems with sizes."

"Okay, men, follow me," Duke said as we walked out to the street. "Guys, we need to take a different train to the Gannon ranch."

"Another train?" Running Bull asked. "Will it take us to our final destination?"

"Almost. Mr. Gannon's caretaker will pick us up at the station in a farm truck and drive us to the ranch—just a couple more miles— that's all."

I looked at our sturdy players and then looked at the elderly Amos.

"You're right." Duke gave me a nod. "I'll telephone Karl and let him know that we've arrived."

I took Amos by the arm so I could escort him to my car. He was much shorter than I, about five-five, but amazingly strong for an elderly man with so little meat on his bones. We took our time, and as we sauntered along in the direction of the parking lot, I realized that including Amos was important. Here was a wise man, a mentor, who had been with the players all of their lives. Of course, the men needed Amos. He was as essential as any of the other players.

"Why do you take medicine?" he asked me.

"My heart is in bad shape. Most of the time it bangs against my chest, reminding me that I'm going to die."

"How soon?"

"Don't really know and neither does my doctor, but it won't be long. The Lord says, *Let not your heart be troubled*, and I'm trying to heed His advice, but it's hard to do. So—tell me, Amos. What made you decide to join the team at the last minute?"

"It wasn't my decision. It was my destiny. After you left our reservation, a heavy feeling came upon me, telling me that I should travel with the team. I didn't tell anyone about this but kept it to myself. So, when the players asked if I would travel with them to California, I knew it was meant to be. It's not wise to fight the strong winds of fate. It was my time and my purpose. For what reason, I may never know."

"*To every thing there is a season, and a time to every purpose under the heaven*," I said.

"Ecclesiastes, chapter three, verse one," Amos said.

When I first saw Amos getting off the train, I was ashamed to admit that my initial reaction was perhaps a little cynical and demeaning. But after the short drive to my ranch, I, too, felt the strong winds of fate telling me that Amos was essential to my team, and that we were destined to be good friends.

~ Chapter Twenty-Three ~

Karl met the men at the Pacific Electric train station near Downey, and after they piled onto the back of the farm truck, he drove Duke and the Lakota players to the ranch. Amos and I arrived a little later, but after the long and exhausting day, everyone was relieved to be at the ranch.

We showed the men the bunkhouse, which also had a small but adequate shower, sink, and commode. They only needed ten beds. The remaining two bunks held stacks of uniforms along with belts, socks, and shoes.

Duke picked up a handful of shirts. "I'd like for everyone to try on a complete uniform. If there are any problems, I've only got tomorrow to make sure everyone is properly attired." He continued to pass out several shirts and pants, and when he got to Amos, he chuckled. "Here you are, sir. You'll wear the number one, since you seem to be the number one guy around here."

I liked that quality in Duke. Everyone, even Amos, was worthy of wearing the Lakota uniform. Amos held up his shirt. "Lakotas" was written across the chest, and on the back a large number.

"You men are now officially known as the *Los Angeles Lakotas*," I announced.

Karl poked his head inside the bunkhouse. "In a few minutes, Ruth will have sandwiches and apple pie for everyone. We're setting up on the upper patio."

"Thanks, Karl," I replied. "We'll be there shortly."

Duke waited until everyone had dressed in their new digs and then wrote down their official number in his notebook. By this time everyone was standing around in their stocking feet, waiting for their shoes. The stiff, black footwear had never been worn, and although the sizes and widths varied, most were too narrow for the players. Duke and I could instantly see they would not be suitable for comfortable play. Blisters and other irritations could potentially inhibit top performances.

"What are we going to do, Phin?" Duke asked. "You know as well as I, the rule book states that shoes must be uniform. I've got three dozen pairs here, but none seem to be wide enough for most of the team."

"Maybe we can soak these new shoes overnight in the water trough," I said. "That might soften and stretch the leather, and it would give the men a full day to break them in."

"We can play in our boots," Running Deer said.

"Boots! Those heavy, clumsy things?" Duke said.

We examined their government-issued footwear. None of their black boots were new but rather ranged in condition from fair to good. Yet, in consideration of the official rules of dress, they were all uniform in color and style.

Duke didn't like the boot idea. "You'll need speed and lots of it," he said. "So how in the world can you run bases or chase down balls wearing these heavy things?"

"Unlike your shoes, our boots are comfortable," center fielder Johnny Chasing Hawk said.

"Certainly you didn't play in boots at the Carlisle School," Duke said.

"We had good shoes, real baseball shoes, that were very comfortable because they were well-worn by other players before us," Chasing Hawk said. "These boots are our winter shoes, and at least they have been broken in."

After running an expense tally in my head for dozens of pairs of shoes, I thought about returning some of them for a refund. I could do this if they were in perfect condition, but any shoes soaked in the trough would be my expense. I had to make some sort of decision. Stiff shoes would not work and neither would boots.

"The official rules don't require us to wear a specific type of shoe," Bill Singing Wolf said. "They only require our shoes to be uniform. After we polish them, everyone will see that they are the same shoe."

"You got a point there," Duke said. "But boots will ruin your game."

I looked at their boots. Even Amos was wearing the same boot. They would satisfy the official dress rule but at what cost to the game?

"Okay, men," I said. "Here's what we'll do. Find the pair of our new shoes that fits best. We'll put those shoes in the trough to soak overnight. Let's hope they'll be supple enough by Sunday. Boots will be our fall back position."

Duke looked at me and scratched his head. "It may look a little strange with their knickers, but I'll not argue with what works."

For years, Duke had wanted to manage a topnotch team of professionals, which in his mind meant there would be no struggles with equipment and uniforms. But as a loyal friend, he stuck with me on this one, trusting that I would have all the right answers. When in reality, I was unsure at every turn. The shoes proved to be one more problem in a string of problems that hindered my efforts. Whether the men wore their boots or their ill-fitting new shoes, their footwear would thwart their chance for a victory, giving Mort's team an unfair advantage. I didn't want to lose under those circumstances and neither did Duke. Our only course was to forge ahead, put on a joyous smile, and pass on some encouraging words.

"I have one more thing I'd like to say before you men grab a bite to eat," Duke said. "We are grateful that you all arrived safely. That's number one. We know you're hoping for a win on Sunday. Phineas and I are hoping for that win as well, but hope is only a substitute for action. We need action on that field. We need your best performance. As you know, you must win that first game, or be prepared to return to South Dakota. So, tonight while you're getting a good rest, think about your personal game. Think about the feel of the ball, how you run, hit, slide, and field. From now on we need to have winning thoughts, and only winning thoughts."

"We will win, coach," Chasing Hawk assured Duke. "We have many families on the reservation who have needs. We want to help them. We want this win more than Mr. Gannon."

"We all want and need this win," Duke said. "I've put my baseball reputation on the line, and Phineas has already invested several thousand dollars just to get you here. I understand your needs back home. I also don't want you to play with heavy family burdens on your minds. I want you to concentrate on your individual game and on your team game. Your opposition is a mixed bag of Major Leaguers and many talented semipros from this region. I've seen the talent around Southern California, and I've played against and along side both National and American League players. They know this sport and play it at its highest level. Even though Mort's Silver Suds players represent years of individual experience, they lack the experience of working as a cohesive team. That's your strong suit. Use it. I know that you men can win because I can see fire in your eyes. Tomorrow we'll focus on basic skills and communication. We have only one day before the game. Let's make the most of it."

I thought about Duke's coaching and leadership style and was satisfied that he was the best coach for this job.

"Okay, men, I think Ruth and Karl are ready for us," I interrupted. "Let's have a bite to eat before turning in for the evening."

I made arrangements to spend the night at the ranch and suggested that Duke stay here as well. But since he lived nearby, his refusal was understandable. I knew he'd be back before sunrise.

During the night, I was restless and uncomfortable. While lying in bed, one, two, then three hours passed. Indigestion seemed to be the cause, but I wasn't certain. Even after a bromo, I still couldn't sleep. As the night hours lingered, one thought led to another. My sour stomach reminded me of my overall ill health and Maggie's future. Her continued happiness would depend upon Paul's ability to carry on with the company.

I began to wonder about my dear friend Mort, whom I had admired for decades. I couldn't imagine why he would break his marriage vows, and for what gain? I was so disappointed in him. Jeanne and Maggie were best friends, and I felt stuck in the middle, forced to keep his vile secret.

Then there was Sunday's baseball game. If my Lakotas fell short of delivering a win, or at the very least a quality game, I would be the laughingstock of Los Angeles, and so would my good friend Duke. I knew he was sticking his neck out for me because of our friendship. But what other manager of note would coach a team of amateur Indians? And what would the baseball community think of my dear friend should we go down in defeat?

With so much on my mind, I donned my robe and slippers and stepped out onto the bedroom balcony that overlooked the backyard. The stars brightened as the nearly full moon dipped low in the sky. I saw the shadowy images of everything I owned—the pool and pool house, my large pasture, the barn. But as my eyes followed the landscape beyond my house, I noticed a man standing in the middle of the yard. He stood motionless with arms outstretched to the heavens.

I decided to see who it was. I knew it was one of my players, but which one? I crept downstairs, so as not to disturb Karl and Ruth, and left through the kitchen and out the backdoor to investigate. As I walked across the lower terrace and down the slope toward the bunkhouse, I realized it was Amos.

"Good evening, Amos," I said in a low voice, far enough away so I wouldn't startle him. "Do you mind if I join you?"

Amos didn't move a muscle but continued to face the heavens. "Please, join me," he said.

I walked over and stood beside him, gazing up as well. "I can see the Big Dipper," I said.

"They are the 'Seven Stars' and represent the seven council fires of the Lakota," Amos replied. *"Seek Him who maketh the seven stars and turneth the shadow of death into the morning, and maketh the day dark with night: that calleth for the waters of the sea, and poureth them out upon the face of the earth: The LORD is his name."*

"Do you often quote scripture while reflecting on your own culture?

"It's from the Book of Amos."

We continued to look up at the big sky, and together, in our own quiet ways, we enjoyed the stillness of the night and the awesomeness of God's creation.

"Are you thinking about Sunday's game and the players?" I asked.

Amos said nothing. I kept still, gazing up at the heavens until he broke the silence.

"These are the same stars that shine over the Pine Ridge Reservation," he said with his wrinkled and weathered face still pointing upward.

How remarkable, I thought. Amos's eyes were obscured by cataracts, but he visualized the stars.

"How much can you see?" I asked.

"Many things. *We walk by faith, not by sight.* Lakota tradition says that stars live on the edge of the universe where no man can reach them. And we should not try, for they are evil and fear the sun."

My friend Amos seemed to be a curiosity, a pagan by heritage, yet a Christian. But then—weren't we all dangerously placing one foot in the world and one foot in the Lord's kingdom? As we continued to admire the heavens, I tried my best to reflect upon my own shortcomings, recalling a verse from the book of Job. *"...lay up His words in your heart. For then we will have delight in the Almighty and lift our faces to God."*

"The Lord asks us to make our prayers known to Him, and He will hear us," Amos said. "We are visitors in this land of California, which offers great opportunities. I thank the Almighty for that blessing."

"Should I ask God for a victory on Sunday, or maybe praying for something so trivial would be taking the Lord's name in vain? Do you think it's okay?"

"Who are we to say what is trivial? And why do we find it so hard to believe that God will provide us with an outcome that is in all of our best interests? I pray for His will to be done."

"But if God can command all of the forces of the universe with the sound of his voice, surely a win on Sunday wouldn't be so difficult."

"Perhaps your desire is not worthy," Amos answered. "It is for God to decide."

We quieted again, and then Amos slowly turned his body like the earth on its rotation. His outstretched arms seemed to feel and absorb his surroundings. He lifted up a soulful chant that gently echoed over the pasture below. It was a prayer of thanksgiving to *Wakan Takan*, the Great Spirit.

"You should try this," he said.

I looked up and lifted my hands toward heaven.

"All things of God are inside the sacred circle of *Hocoka*," he said. "Just like a compass, there are four directions. *Waziyatakiva* is North and white. It is for the wisdom gained through winter. *Itokagata is South and yellow. It is for vegetation and represents our innocence. Wiyohiyanpata is East and red. It is for the sunrise and our new found enlightenment. Wiyohpeyata is West and black. It is about storms and their power. Altogether t*hey represent the seasons, completeness, and the stages of mankind."

"Do you think about dying?" I asked.

"I'm an old man, and we know God will keep us here on earth until we've accomplished His will. Are you afraid of dying?"

"No—only afraid of dying too soon. Maggie wants to see Europe, and it would be nice if I were available to help my nephew at Gannon

Fine Meats when he hits his first major catastrophe." It dawned on me that I hadn't shared these thoughts on dying with anyone else, and yet I found the sensitive subject easy to discuss with Amos. "Sunday's game will be my final competition against Mort. It would be serendipitous to have more, but my soul is thinking out loud and telling me that this one's our last." I drew a deep breath and exhaled slowly, hoping for one last victory before I should die.

"And your wife, what does she say about this?"

"It's difficult. I can talk to Maggie about everything, except my death, though we dance around the subject. My passing means our separation. I imagine it would give her great sorrow. Will she be lonely? Will she feel safe and secure being totally dependent on our nephew? It's all so agonizing to think about."

Amos was quiet as he soaked in all of my random thoughts. And then he had these comforting words. *"Consider the ravens: for they neither sow nor reap; which neither have storehouse nor barn; and God feeds them.* Aren't your wife and nephew better than the fowls of the earth?"

Amos was right. Paul and Maggie were indeed in good hands. My friends Mort and Duke have been a blessing to me. Mort kept my mind stimulated with fresh ideas, and Duke reminded me that hard work and patience pay off in the end, but Amos was the comforting friend I needed at this time in my life. He brought me peace.

"We are alike, you and I, a brotherhood," Amos said. "There is a fine Lakota word, *tiospaye.* It means we are all related."

I felt that kindred spirit as I continued to look up at the stars in my robe and slippers, slowly turning my body. There we were—two grown men in the center of the yard, in the middle of the night, with our arms outstretched, reaching for the heavens—Amos saying a prayer in his native tongue, and I praying silently. We both needed God's grace and wisdom.

~ CHAPTER TWENTY-FOUR ~

The following day I met the players and Amos on the upper patio for breakfast. Duke had already arrived and joined the men for a hearty meal before our only day of practice. It was a clear day, although precipitation was not totally unexpected. After all, November was on the cusp of Southern California's rainy season. But blue skies prevailed and were forecasted for the entire weekend.

"Karl, I'd like you to put Pork Chop in the bull pen," I said. "The cows can stay in the lower pasture."

"Pork Chop will be fine for now," Duke said. "We'll practice near the barn this morning. How are the shoes?"

"Oh, yes, the shoes," I said. "I don't believe they've been retrieved from the water trough."

"It's just as well," Duke reassured me. "The men should put them on wet so they'll stretch and mold to their feet. I'd like to start with some light running drills. That will tell us everything we need to know about the shoes."

When we finished our breakfast, sorting the shoes was our first priority. At first, no one was sure which pair was theirs, but after trading this one for that, they worked it out. The shoes did stretch somewhat but remained much too tight, though everyone was able to lace up.

Duke pulled a small ball of string from his pocket and placed one end under a small rock.

"Here's your starting line," he said, making a long mark in the soil with a stick. He completely unraveled the string while walking away. At the other end, he made a second mark on the ground, parallel to the first. "And here is your finish line."

I knew exactly what he planned to do the moment he handed me one of his two stopwatches. I would clock the slowest runner, and he would clock the first man to cross the finish line.

"I don't know how fast you men had to run in order to make a single at Carlisle, but I know exactly how fast you must run to get a single tomorrow."

The players got into position, and Duke and I stood at the finish line with our stopwatches ready to clock the times. Then with a swift drop of his arm and a loud "GO!" Karl gave the signal for the men to start running and for us to start our timepieces.

I thought the players were impressive as they darted across the yard. Then with a click...click, Duke and I stopped the watches at the appropriate times. Center fielder Johnny Chasing Hawk was first to cross the line, and pitcher David Eagle Eye was last.

Duke looked at his watch, and then he looked at mine.

"That wasn't bad," he said, "but the three men who came in last need to cut their times. Johnny, you were the lead runner, and your speed was okay, even for a Major League pro, but if you can cut it down further, then everyone else will have a faster time as well. Okay, men, line up again."

I pulled Duke aside while the men took their positions. "Maybe they could shave off a second, but twenty percent? That would be a miracle."

"And that's exactly what we need—a miracle. Once our players reach that faster speed, they'll have a chance at a base hit, and maybe the possibility of stretching it into a double. But if this is all of the speed these guys can muster, then get your bank draft ready for Mort because you'll be writing him one hefty check."

Duke and I cleared our stopwatches, and everyone got in position for round two. Then once again Karl gave the signal as he shouted, "Go!" The players took off running.

Click…click. We stopped our watches as they crossed the finish line. I handed mine over to Duke.

After a long pause, Duke looked at me and then he faced the men. "This is very impressive. I've never known any man who could cut so much time off his speed, but I still need you to run a little faster."

"I can," Johnny said, panting.

"Oh?" I said.

"Yes," he replied. "Just let me go barefoot."

"Sorry, you can't do that," Duke said.

"Then let me wear my boots."

I looked down at Johnny's feet. His smallest toes had punched through the sides of his shoes. Other players had similar complaints. So, as peculiar as their boots would appear when worn with knickers, it was obvious they would be part of the official uniform. It was not a good solution, but it was our only option, so the men put on their boots.

For the next drill we asked the men to swing, put the bat down, and run the same distance. Duke would clock the men, and I would write down their times. This would help Duke decide the best batting order possible.

Johnny went first. He swung his bat, put it down, and ran like a bullet flying out of a gun, crossing the finish line at top speed.

Duke looked at his stopwatch and showed it to me. "If Johnny runs this fast tomorrow, he ought to be able to steal a few bases."

I began to feel, with some sense of relief, that maybe, just maybe, Duke and I wouldn't be considered complete fools at tomorrow's game. But running was only one small part of the test. There were other skills we wanted to measure in order to understand their level of play.

For this we needed Pork Chop penned. It was highly possible that balls would fall into the lower pasture, so as a precaution, I had Karl lure the bull into the corral with some tempting hay. It didn't matter that a few of Pork Chop's girlfriends followed. At least my bull wouldn't be a threat to the team.

After Duke and a few players measured the distance between the plate and the rubber, the men lined up to bat, and one by one, Duke sized up their batting skills by pitching to every player.

"What do you think?" I asked Duke after every man had his turn at bat.

"It's hard to tell. I think we have good hitters here. I can't pitch as fast or as accurately as I once could, but they all seem to have good form."

"Let's watch David Eagle Eye show off his stuff to a few of the best batters," I suggested.

"I dunno," Duke said. "With Eagle Eye as our only pitcher, I don't want him straining his arm. I only want him doing warm-up pitches."

"Do you think you've had enough time with these guys?"

"Enough to make a batting order, but even so, I'm relying on a lots of hunches. As far as this team is concerned, this is it until game time. I've asked the men to do more calisthenics later today and tomorrow morning. I'll stop by the ranch around noon after worship services."

"I wish you and the team all the best," I said, shaking Duke's hand in appreciation, knowing that he was staking his pride and reputation on Sunday's performance.

"I'll see you men tomorrow," he replied as he waved goodbye to me and the players.

"I want to crush the white man at the ballpark," Running Deer said.

But his comment displeased Amos.

"Tomorrow our Lakota people will have a chance to be great warriors in a white man's game," he responded. "A Lakota knows how to kill, skin, and prepare an animal for sustenance, whereas, there are many white men who only know how to kill, as they did with the buffalo and thousands of our people. But there are also many great white men like McKinley who first taught you how to play baseball, and Mr. Gannon who gave you this opportunity in California. A wise Lakota knows the difference between men of honor and men of shame. If our goal is to simply crush the white man tomorrow, then we will not take home a worthy victory or an honorable defeat. Our goal is to demonstrate our skills and to prove that we can compete."

With every hour in his presence, I grew fonder of Amos. He heightened the spiritual side of my being, which gave me peace. He showed me that it was just as important as anything physical. I began to understand what he meant when he quoted the Bible saying ... *seeing they did not see, and hearing they did not hear.* Amos was truly a wise man who saw and heard beyond the obvious. It was fascinating and humbling to be in his presence.

I left the ranch within the hour and headed back to Los Angeles. Tomorrow would be our big day.

~ CHAPTER TWENTY-FIVE ~

As the sunlight streamed into our bedroom windows on Carroll Avenue, I lay motionless, following the movements of a common housefly buzzing around the room. It dashed from one side to another, without a care in the world, until it found rest on my left cheek. A reactive backhand knocked it to the floor—all six feet upright.

Feeling twinges of guilt, I thought about what I had just done. And as I continued staring at the insect over the edge of the bed, it reminded me of my own mortality. For the betterment of civil society, I strove to live a life of honest virtue, helping others whenever possible, and perhaps accomplishing something notable along the way. But like the deceased fly on the floor, my life would suddenly be over. I supposed everyone loses the race against time, leaving behind some unfinished business. I had lots of unfinished business, but my deepest desire upon passing would be for eternal life after burial honors far exceeding that of a common housefly.

"Sorry, fly. A broom and a dustpan—that's all you get."

I leaned over and kissed Maggie on her shoulder. "Good morning, my sweet."

She moaned awake. "You win. My eyes are open."

"I love winning!" I pulled her close.

"I may be in your arms, darling, but I know you're not thinking of me."

She was right. My mind was on the baseball game, so I switched thoughts to be more truthful. "Not thinking of you while touching your soft skin and smelling your sweetly perfumed hair?"

"I'm not fooled."

After thirty years of marriage, she knew I couldn't hide anything from her, especially on this all-important game day when beating Mort filled every cavity of my brain.

I looked at Maggie. The morning light cast a warm glow over her delicate features. She was as radiant as she was on the first morning of our honeymoon. Rather than jumping out of bed, I took a few moments to gaze at her beauty—her beautiful hair and her lovely breasts, shapes that I could detect through her form-fitting silk nightgown. It was an image of lovely Maggie that I would always remember and one deserving of a gentle kiss.

"Good morning, my love."

Her eyes fluttered. "It is a good morning, a beautiful morning every time I wake up with you by my side."

Sundays had always been special to Maggie and me. We were always alone. Our domestic help was off for the day, so we made our own coffee and lounged around the house, until it was time to ready ourselves for church. Only this week Maggie and I would attend an early worship service to accommodate my game time schedule.

"Are you hungry?" she asked.

"Of course, but not as much as usual. My stomach is tied up in knots."

"Don't worry, darling. I'm sure Morton is feeling quite the same."

"What would you say if I made this my last competition with Mort?"

"I would say, and Jeanne would agree, that you would make two wives very happy. But I suspect we would end up with two very unhappy husbands. What other pastime could give you as much pleasure?"

"Perhaps I could write about all of my crazy competitions with Mort. That would make an interesting book! I've named my team the Los Angeles Lakotas. It has a nice ring to it. Don't you agree?"

"Of course, darling. Now, what would you like for breakfast?"

"I'll have a soft-boiled egg, a slice of toast, and a cup of coffee. The doctor said I must eat less so I can lose some of my midsection. It's mostly in preparation for all the fine dining we'll enjoy in Europe."

"Are you up for such a trip?"

"I don't know. But let's suppose I am. Which country would you like to visit first?"

"England, although I'd love to see Ireland, too—and then we should travel to France and Italy. It's all so exciting."

I noticed how Maggie's face lit up. She was dreaming big of our great voyage, pretending that my body would last for many years to come.

How long can we stay?" she asked.

"Until we tire of the place or the natives beg us to leave."

"I have several brochures on the various countries, and many of the ladies at the women's club have offered some exciting suggestions. Phineas, I'm so looking forward to your retirement and enjoying our golden years together."

It gave me joy to see my wife so happy. I, too, wanted to spend many more years with her, but just as Maggie knew my thoughts on competition day, I knew hers. Deep down inside she knew that our future together would not happen, and every goodbye could be our last.

We left the house around 9:15 a.m. I felt unusually distracted while driving that morning. Worse yet, I couldn't concentrate on the sermon. I didn't want my mind to wander during the pastor's homily, but it did. This day, of all days, I needed the Lord's blessing.

What would I do if my Lakotas lost? I agonized over this question throughout the church service. It had occurred to me from the first moment I saw my ballplayers and their poor conditions at Pine Ridge. If they should lose, and I sent them home, it would cut my losses. On the other hand, I felt I had a responsibility to my team. I wrestled with these concerns until Maggie nudged my side.

"Hymn 482, darling. Our closing song is number 482."

"Yes, yes of course." I flipped to the correct page and began singing...*Jesus, Savior, pilot me.*

After services, Maggie and I went straight home. I was just inside the front door, my hat still on my head, when the telephone began ringing.

"It's for you, darling," Maggie said, handing me the telephone. "It's Karl."

"Yes, Karl. What can I do for you?"

"It's been very busy around here," Karl explained.

Maggie knew I was receiving awful news, so she remained nearby. For the next few minutes, she watched as I listened in horror until my heart began to pound inside my chest *thud, thud-thud, thud-thud.*

"Take this seat," she insisted, scooting the hall chair by my side.

As I continued listening to Karl, my chest pains were almost unbearable. I reached for my pill vial. Maggie took it from me, opened the cork stopper, and shook out some pills into her palm. I quickly swallowed one and then another.

"Tell me, darling, what happened?" Maggie begged me. "Can I get you anything?"

"No," I said as I hung up the phone. "Just help me to my parlor chair. Come, sit with me, and I'll give you the news."

Earlier that morning, Karl and Ruth wiped the heavy dew off the outdoor furniture and readied the upper terrace for breakfast. They brought out several large platters of food and placed them along the buffet table. Karl rang the farm bell, and the players began to gradually appear for their morning meal.

"You men will need a hearty breakfast," Ruth told the players. "I've got pancakes, cream chipped beef gravy, scrambled eggs, and fruit on the buffet table. If you need more to eat, let me know, and I'll bring out more."

Caring for so many guests was a large undertaking for Karl and Ruth. But even with the added work, they wanted the players to do well against Mort's team.

"Please, help yourself," Karl told Chasing Hawk, as he handed him a plate.

"Thank you," he replied and then piled his plate high with food.

"I don't think the weather will get much above seventy today," Karl said, "so it will be a nice day for a game."

"I like California. South Dakota is much colder in November," Chasing Hawk said. "And yet at home we have played in November as well."

While many of the men stayed for second helpings, others decided to loosen their muscles and walk the grounds of the ranch. That was what Duke instructed the men to do—light calisthenics.

Karl was so busy helping Ruth that he had forgotten to make sure Pork Chop was out of harms way. He dropped what he was doing and ran toward the lower pasture. "Look out men!" he yelled. "Pork Chop—I didn't put him in the pen!"

It was always necessary to keep one eye on Pork Chop when taking a stroll around the ranch, and it was never wise to get close to the herd. If Pork Chop got a notion that a stranger was showing an interest in one of his lovely cows, he was likely to get testy. In which case, no one could keep the chivalrous bull away from his fair maidens.

Pete Charging Horse had the misfortune of straying from the others and in the direction of some of the grazing cows. He took his eye off Pork Chop, and in an instant, the bull seized the opportunity to ram him from behind, shoving him to the ground.

Karl ran as hard as he could in the direction of the herd, but he was too late. He saw the incident, scooped up two handfuls of loose dirt, and hurled them at the bull's eyes, distracting him long enough to allow the other teammates to carry the injured Pete to the bunkhouse.

Amos stood over Pete as he lay on his bed. The other players waited nearby for news about Pete. He was in no condition to play, which presented a more serious situation. Without all nine players, the Lakotas would be obliged to forfeit the game, a league position, and their potential earnings for their tribe.

Karl looked at Pete, who could barely lift his head. He knew Pete needed a doctor, but Dr. Burton was in church. Without hesitation, Karl hopped into the farm truck and set out to find him.

About thirty minutes later, both Karl and Dr. Burton returned.

The doctor took his time and carefully examined Pete.

"There doesn't appear to be anything broken," Dr. Burton said. "Only abrasions and one heck of a bruise. But to be sure, Pete needs to stay in bed today."

"What about today's game?" Karl asked.

"He can't play," Doctor Burton insisted, "and that's my final word. I know you athletes. You're always wanting to play with injuries, but this man needs at least three days of rest. I'll examine him again on Wednesday, so have him stop by my office then. And for this man's sake, if his condition gets worse, call me immediately."

"I guess I had better telephone Mr. Gannon," Karl said. "He's not going to be happy to hear this."

And that was when Karl called. I looked at my pocket watch. It was almost noon. Eleven o'clock services were ending, and Duke would soon be at the ranch. Where was Duke going to get another player? He would have to play for Pete. It was the only reasonable solution. Duke's fifty-year-old plus muscles would be sore tonight, and he would be extremely sore with me for not hiring more players.

Maggie took my hand. "Oh, Phin, what are you going to do?"

"At the moment, nothing. If Duke needs my advice, he'll call. No sense making any decisions for him. That's why he's the manager. And if he doesn't call by one o'clock, I'll leave for the ballpark as planned."

~ Chapter Twenty-Six ~

There was no call from Duke, so I drove over to Fiesta Park. I had a hunch he would place his name on our official roster because it had to be turned in upon the team's arrival. This left no time to fill the last spot with anyone else but Duke. I also thought about his earlier words of needing at least twelve players. I certainly deserved the biggest scolding he could thrust upon me.

As I neared the front gate of the ballpark, I noticed his Silver Suds employees handing out samples of soap, each about half the size of a regular bar but individually boxed. Mort spared no expense. Inside every package was a baseball card of one of his Suds players. I was amazed at the size of the crowd. Mort and I both wanted thousands of people on hand to watch our competitions, and without massive numbers of fans, Mort would never be a contender.

"Buy a ticket today, and get a free bar of soap with a baseball card," his pitchmen shouted. I was quite sure Mort employed other methods to fill the stadium, because as I entered the park, I noticed that nearly every seat was taken—quite unusual for a preseason event and very unusual one hour before game time. If I should lose today, the large crowd would at least soften my losses, though my share of the day's purse would only put a small dent in my overall costs.

"Mr. Gannon!" a familiar voice shouted.

I looked around and didn't see anyone in particular.

"Mr. Gannon!" the voice shouted again.

I looked again and saw Travis Maxwell weaving his way through the crowd.

"Well, I'll be. I guess you were able to talk your publisher into a California getaway."

We smiled and exchanged handshakes.

"This time of year California sure beats Denver. I guess you're all excited about today's game?"

"You can't possibly imagine all the excitement this team has given me," I replied.

"I know our readers will love the follow-up stories I've planned. Your travels to South Dakota will appear in our next issue, and the following month we'll feature this game."

I didn't tell Maxwell that our team was in serious trouble with one man short. He'd soon learn of Pete Charging Horse's accident, and I was in no condition to repeat the upsetting news.

"Do you have time for a few more questions?" Maxwell asked.

"Not now, but after the game. I promise. We'll get together then."

Maxwell headed for the press booth, and I walked over to our Lakota side and stepped down into the dugout. There, on the bench, sat Duke.

"Hello, Phin," Duke said with no eye contact. His head didn't turn one inch. He just looked forward at the infield.

I sat down next to him.

"We have a bit of a problem," Duke said.

"I know. I heard about Pete. Karl phoned me this morning."

"Phin, it's my fault," Duke said. "When I suggested that the men do a light workout this morning, I didn't think they would go near the lower pasture where your livestock was grazing."

"Is Pete okay?" I asked.

"Dr. Burton gave him some painkillers. He doesn't believe anything's broken, and he'll probably be able to play next Sunday—

that is, if we're lucky enough to have a game next Sunday. But today, we're one man short."

"I figured that much."

Duke looked despondent, and I could understand why.

"At first I thought this would be a nightmare for us," he said. "But hear me out, Phin."

"I know. I've been thinking hard about this whole situation as well, and I'm sorry that you'll have to play."

"But that's the issue. I'm not playing. Amos is our ninth man."

"What?" I was dumbfounded. "Don't tell me that!"

"I just did, and Amos is in the lineup."

"Duke, that's crazy! You must play for Pete. That way, if we lose, this crowd will at least get an opportunity to watch the return of the great Duke Maner. Even I would buy a ticket for that, and I wouldn't need one of Mort's soap samplers to convince me."

Duke didn't say a word, which made me realize there was more to this story.

"What makes you think Amos is capable of playing ball?" I asked. "He'll get hurt out there."

"Don't be sore," Duke said. "There's a good reason why he's substituting for Pete."

"That's preposterous! Amos can't play. He can barely see, and his running pace is the same as his walk. Does the league president know about this yet?"

"Well, yes and no. Amos is on the roster, but they won't know who he is until the game's underway. The umpires will immediately request a time out and a conference. They'll call me out onto the field to explain the elderly player. I'll argue the rule book and win."

"And what makes you so sure?"

"Look at the size of this crowd. The umpires won't want a riot on their hands. Mort did a great job filling the ballpark, and it's the very thing that will prevent a forfeit, especially when we're technically in the right."

"Your decision makes a mockery of the sport." I patted my breast in search of my medicine bottle. "Oh, dear! Where are my pills?" I panicked, but calmed when I remembered they were in my pants pocket. My hands were trembling as I opened the vial.

"Do you need water?" Duke asked.

"No, I don't need water. I just need to know why you made this outlandish decision."

I soon realized that Duke had no choice once he explained.

After Dr. Burton left the ranch, the men carried Pete up to the house and put him in the guest bedroom. Amos was by his side when Duke darted into the room.

"Amos!" he cried out. "How's Pete?"

Amos stood up. "Bad—very bad."

"I just spoke with Running Bull and a few other players," Duke explained. "It looks as though I'll have to play." But Duke also knew we would need the tribal elder's approval. "If I play first base and the first baseman moves to third, it would allow me to substitute for the pitcher should Eagle Eye tire late in the game."

Amos fell silent.

Duke couldn't tell if Amos was contemplating the substitution or if his idea was objectionable. He waited a few moments longer for Amos's response.

"Amos, please!" he pleaded. "It's a good solution."

While staring deep into Duke's eyes, he asked, "Are you Lakota?"

"No, I'm afraid not." All Duke could think about was the worst case scenario, a forfeited game."

"If you're not Lakota, then you don't play," Amos insisted. "Only Lakota play on a Lakota team."

"But be reasonable," Duke said. "Where are we going to get another Lakota baseball player in Los Angeles?"

"I am Lakota," Amos said proudly. "He returned to Pete's bedside and asked him. "Can you tell me about third base? I need to know how to play that position."

Pete moaned. "What? You want to take my place?"

"Yes, I must play for you."

Pete never questioned the wisdom of Amos, but practically speaking, he was not hopeful of the outcome. For Duke the cultural divide was widening, and he feared Amos's substitution was the team's only hope for survival.

"There is no time to pause at third base," Pete spoke softly so he could continue with shallow breaths. "You must never take your eyes off of the ball because third base is an instant reaction position."

Amos repeated Pete's words to himself. He knew it wouldn't matter whether his milky eyes were on or off the ball. He trembled. "Tell me more," Amos insisted, knowing that his age and poor vision were deadly handicaps for a third baseman, but forfeiting the game was not an option for Amos or his people.

Pete continued, "At third base the ball rarely soars in your direction; it projects swiftly through the air as if it were a charging buffalo. It may hit you directly in the chest or on a first bounce. Your job is to stop the ball when it is barely visible. You must also watch Eagle Eye at the mound and our catcher Running Bull behind home plate."

"Why?" Amos asked.

"When the signal is given for a change up, the ball will probably pull in your direction."

Duke was stunned and thought, surely the old man didn't want to participate in the game, but then, maybe he did.

Amos asked Duke to close the door. Only the three men were in the room when Amos began to sing a prayer. It was a mournful song that went on and on—almost too long.

Duke looked at his watch. There was no more time to spare.

He took Amos by the arm. "We'll have to go. There's just enough time to get to the park. Don't worry about Pete. Karl and Ruth will look after him."

The team loaded the farm truck with their gear and hopped into the back. Amos rode in the front with Duke, who wanted to use the time together to talk about the roster and maybe change Amos's mind about playing. But it was fruitless.

Amos chanted some gibberish most of the way and started singing a native melody when they reached the outskirts of Los Angeles. He appeared almost trancelike while singing.

"That's some tune you got there," Duke said as he continued to drive.

Amos didn't respond. As the team neared the downtown area, traffic became more congested, and at a stop sign, Duke had to hit the brakes to keep from rear-ending another car. The truck jerked forward. Amos nearly slid off his seat.

"Sorry, Amos, I didn't expect traffic to be this heavy." Worried about the other players, Duke poked his head out the window and shouted, "Is everyone okay back there?"

"We're fine," one of the players shouted back.

"It won't be much farther," Duke said, relieved that all of his men were okay.

He parked three blocks from the stadium—the closet spot he could find for the truck. He helped Amos out of his seat as the other players hopped off the back.

"Running Deer, I'm going to put you and Amos in a taxi. Fiesta Park is not far from here, but I can't afford to lose any more players before the game."

Running Deer took Amos by the arm, and Duke hailed a taxi.

"Where to?" the cabbie asked.

"Fiesta Park," Duke replied as he handed the fare to the driver. "Meet us at the front gate."

Running Deer helped Amos into the cab. Seeing all of the Indians dressed in baseball uniforms must have seemed odd to the cabbie. "You ballplayers aren't from around here, are you?" the he asked.

"No, we're from South Dakota," Running Deer replied.

"And you're gonna play winter ball here in L.A. against the Major League pros?" The cabbie's voice was rude and cynical.

"Yeah, at two o'clock," Duke said. "If you can get off work, you ought to buy a ticket."

"I don't think I can, but I can definitely see that it'll be an interesting game."

After the taxi pulled away from the curb, Duke looked at the remaining players and pointed up the street. "Follow me. An invigorating walk will do you good and loosen up your joints, especially mine."

Once everyone met up at the front gate, Duke escorted the men inside the park to the Lakota dugout on the third base line.

"This is it, men," Duke said. "You'll have some time to loosen up on the field, and then the game will begin. I wish you all the best. I know that you'll be putting your heart and soul into this effort, so let's hope those thoughts will turn into a victory. Now get out there and start looking like Major Leaguers."

After the men headed out to the field for their warm up, leaving Duke and Amos sitting on the bench, Duke took out a folded paper from his pocket.

"Amos, in my hand I'm holding our official roster which must be turned in now. I know my bones are a bit stiff, but I'm in good health. Certainly my experience must be considered as we make our final decision on the lineup. Now I can leave my name on this official roster, or I can substitute yours. Whose name shall it be?"

"Duke," Amos replied, "if we win this game with you as a player, my Lakota people don't really win."

"But, Amos, it's perfectly legitimate."

"Legitimate, perhaps, but win or lose, we can't go back to South Dakota with honor if you play with our Lakota men. This is our first game against professional white men, so why would we want a white man on our team?"

"Now that, my dear friend, is quite an honorable attitude. Unfortunately, today in this park it's going to be declared an act of great stupidity."

"The white man has much difficulty understanding the ways of the Lakota."

Duke listened carefully to Amos's words, trying to be as polite as possible.

"We have already won by being here today, off the reservation, showing the white man we are baseball warriors fully capable of going into battle. As Lakota, we would never want to forfeit that honor."

"Look, I don't want to spoil that unique win of yours, but it appears that Phineas and I have just forfeited this game, while you and your men take that unusual Lakota victory back to South Dakota on tomorrow's train."

"We won't lose. Our Lakota team is very good."

"But, Amos, you don't understand. Mort's team is full of men from Major League clubs. There's phenomenal talent over there in that other dugout. This is not a sandlot game you're about to play." Duke threw his hands into the air to emphasize his frustration. "Do you see the thousands of spectators in the stands? They paid fifty cents to see this game." Duke realized that he had misspoken. "How silly of me! Of course, you don't see them, but that ought to scare you to death!"

188

"I'm not fearful of other baseball warriors."

"Fear is not the issue here!" Duke raised his voice. "It's the ability to win. Without Pete, we're playing with both hands tied behind our backs."

"To have no faith is an insult to God and to our team."

It was now quite clear that Amos would not relinquish his position on the team, and it was futile for Duke to continue. To Amos, the team and Lakota honor were more important than any individual player.

"Okay, Amos. I apologize." Duke backed off, realizing the elder tribesman's decision was not negotiable. "Perhaps I was a bit offensive suggesting that I could substitute for a Lakota, and now that you've explained this team honor angle, you're gonna get to play today." Duke shook his head in disbelief. "But you'll have to play where I put you, and it's not third base."

"Not third base?"

"No, Amos, not third base. Standing there will kill you! Then we'd really lose. This is gonna be a heck of a challenge for a coach, and it's gonna push all of the other Lakota players to try much harder, but this is your game. Win or lose, as you put it. I just don't know how Phin will take this." Duke placed his hand on his chest. "I sure hope he has lots of pills with him today."

"We will play a good game today. These men have played many good games and can promise one today," Amos assured Duke. "As for me, I am only one Lakota, and one Lakota does not make an entire tribe."

"Well said," Duke replied with sarcasm. "I'm glad you're ready."

Listening to Duke made me realize how important an all-Lakota team was to Amos and to the rest of the players. Amos was willing to put his life on the line for his team, his tribe, and his Indian nation.

But as I listened to Duke explain the details, I also knew that Amos's decision to be a substitute for Pete Charging Horse had not only thrown the game to Mort, but it would be a great embarrassment to both Duke and me the moment the crowds noticed Amos on the field.

"So you see, Phin," Duke said at the conclusion of his story, "I had no choice. All I could do was remove the pencil from behind my ear, erase my name from the roster, and substitute the name *Amos Wise Heart.* If we don't go forward with this game now, every one of these fans will want their money back, and the league will probably ask you for some additional compensation for the embarrassment."

"I'm sorry—it looks as though he'll have to play."

"I placed Amos in right field. It's the safest place for him, and let's hope he doesn't interfere with the other players. Bill Singing Wolf is now on third. Amos bats last."

"Undoubtedly, we'll be forced to forfeit an out every time he's at the plate," I said. "That is, of course, if the opposing pitcher doesn't injure him first. This is unbelievable—a nearly blind man on a baseball team."

"At least he can see well enough to find home plate," Duke said.

"This all boils down to honor—Lakota honor."

"Lakota honor? What about my honor? What about your honor?" Duke stood up, stepped out of the dugout, and faced the crowd. "Look at this stadium. It's nearly full. After today's game, we may never be welcomed back to Fiesta Park ever—not even in the cheap seats!"

"I don't like this situation any more than you, but this was the hand we were dealt, so let's play it the best we can."

"Phin, we've been friends a long time. I know that you're out of shape, that you're popping pills to stay alive, and that this game will probably be your last competition against Mort. So, I'll stick by you today, even though I know how the *Los Angeles Times* and the *Herald* will embarrass me in tomorrow's papers. But that's how I define honor."

~ CHAPTER TWENTY-SEVEN ~

Mort had just arrived at the park. He was a little late, but in time for the coin toss, a tribute reserved for team owners. When the umpire called for us to approach home plate, I saw Mort staring at my players. He was wearing a smirk that stretched across his face as he walked onto the field.

"Phineas, where in the world did you find that team?" Mort chortled.

"I thought you knew, South Dakota. They're Lakota Sioux, and they're going to surprise you plenty today."

"You got that right." Mort slapped me on the back. "They are surprising!"

"This is only a qualifying game," the umpire announced. "The winning team shall be awarded the last slot in the Los Angeles Winter Ball League. So, gentlemen, what shall it be?"

"Heads," Mort quickly shouted.

The silver dollar rose high into the air, tumbling several times before landing by the umpire's feet.

"Tails it is."

"Looks like I've won the first round." I smiled and allowed my eyes to twinkle at Mort while he bristled. "We're naturally batting last."

"It only means we're playing nine full innings," he snarled. "I'll see you in the stands."

After the toss, Duke and I returned to the dugout.

"This is it, men," Duke declared to our players. "We won the toss. Amos, you'll need to head out to the field." He looked around and put his hand on Chasing Hawk's shoulder. "Take Amos out to right and plant him ten feet inside the foul line so he doesn't accidently step outside. Make sure he's not too deep so he won't have much walking to do, and most of all, pick a spot where he'll be out of your way. You and Buffalo Warrior will need to cover all three fields. You'll have some help from second base."

"And where is that second baseman Tom Fighting Bear?" I asked.

"He's on the field," Chasing Hawk replied.

"Well...I'm sure he knows that you need all the help you can get," Duke said. "That's a tall order for the three of you. A good fielder can cover his position and a little extra, but it will take an additional effort to cover that much territory in the outfield. Good luck out there."

Johnny Chasing Hawk helped Amos to his feet and continued holding him for balance as he teetered up the dugout steps.

"Amos, wait," Duke said. "Are you right-handed or left?"

Amos wasn't sure of the question.

"It doesn't matter. I only have a right-hander's glove available. Here, hold out your hand." Duke helped Amos put on the glove. "At least you'll look the part—sort of. Just stand wherever Chasing Hawk places you, and for goodness sake, don't move and don't worry about the ball."

Duke turned to his pitcher David Eagle Eye. "Okay, Eagle Eye, Pee-Wee Coltrain's the leadoff batter. It'll sting to have him make it to first, knowing the heart of the batting order will be right behind him. Pee-Wee was an outstanding rookie this year in Detroit—batted almost .300 for the season. I wish I knew more about him, but if I were coaching Mort's team, I'd probably have him batting first, too. It's your game out there, Eagle Eye. Is your arm ready?"

"Yes, it's been ready for a long time. Professional ball was only a dream for us when we played at the Carlisle School, and now we're here. We thank you." He gave Duke and me a half smile and jogged out to the mound.

The National Anthem would soon play so the game could begin, but in the meantime, some of the crowd had formed unfavorable opinions once they caught sight of Amos. With every slow and careful step Chasing Hawk and Amos took toward right field, the fans became increasingly loud—laughing, mocking as if they had every right to criticize our players. I could only imagine the painful humiliation the Lakota players must have felt. Duke felt it, too. By the time Chasing Hawk safely positioned Amos along the foul line, jeers and boos echoed around the ballpark.

Duke returned to the bench and removed his cap. After massaging his temples, he hooked the cap back onto his head. "This is a nightmare for us, Phin."

Duke was correct with his assessment. We had no true picture of their skill level other than my brief observation and Travis Maxwell's article, and now our Lakotas were about to be put to the test. Losing this game would be devastating to Duke and me, and there was nothing more we could do, only hope that our pitcher would spare us further embarrassment by lasting all nine innings.

"I'm sorry I talked you into this," I told Duke.

"Don't worry about it. I knew exactly what I was getting into. Los Angles club owners don't want a local pitcher like me managing their Major League players. They want a big league guy to head up their clubs. I guess I wanted to manage a team so much that it didn't really matter at the time what kind of players they'd be. I suppose I was a little too eager to help you with your dream because it was feeding mine."

"Maybe that's how it all started, but here we are. Good luck, Duke," I said. "I'm heading for the stands."

It was bad enough that both Duke and I would be the biggest losers of the day, but reporters from both major Los Angles newspapers would no doubt sensationalize the game and make us appear as fools in tomorrow's editions. It was all I could think about on my way up into the grandstand.

Mort and I had adjoining front row box seats, slightly to the right of home plate. As I took my seat, I acknowledged Mort in a friendly way and waited for his snide remark about Amos.

"Looks like grandpa's playing right field. I hope he's had his afternoon nap so he can last all nine innings." Mort laughed out loud. "It's the craziest thing I've ever seen, and for your sake, I hope he doesn't get hurt."

I kept up a false front of confidence, knowing full well that our Lakotas were vulnerable in so many ways. I positioned myself in my normal, casual way, slouching slightly in my seat with my legs stretched long.

Mort sat upright, looking far too analytical for a ballgame. He usually turned sport into more work than pleasure, and for this game he was completely immersed in paperwork. Statistics and player histories covered his lap.

"Why do you go to such trouble?" I asked. "There's only $500 riding on today's game, not $5,000."

Mort looked up. "I'm planning for next week's game."

"Don't waste your time."

"Ha! Have you even seen your team? They look as if they dressed at a church rummage sale. Really now, Phin, boots as part of the uniform!"

"If your employees could only see how you slave over baseball stats, perhaps they'd understand your compulsion to analyze every bubble in your factory."

"Winning is all about statistics. Whether its baseball or business, it makes no difference. By using these games to launch new products and properly marketing existing lines, I gain far more than an afternoon of sparring with you. The publicity this team will generate when my men go into the playoffs should move boxes and boxes of soap all around the southland. Every barber and drugstore will want to stock my product, and men wouldn't dare travel without it!"

"But why should you be the one keeping tabs on the players? Isn't that a job for your overpaid manager from Boston? Besides, you have to win today's trial, so all of your paper shuffling will be meaningless after this game."

"I suppose you're right about the stats," Mort said, as he placed his papers in the seat next to him. "It's all in the hands of our coaches and players."

"That's right, so sit back and enjoy the game. I have a good feeling about my Lakotas. I suppose the City of Azusa could possibly squeeze your team into their league at this late date. Then you'll be known as the *Azusa Silver Suds.* " I laughed out loud. "The Azusa Silver Suds. That has a nice sound. I can just see your team's initials on the official scorecard—A-S-S."

Mort snorted. "At least my Suds have marketing potential. What product is your Lakota team going to move? I know!" Mort held up a solitary index finger. "How about importing some buffalo?" He chortled. "You could say *a tough team and a tough meat.*"

I didn't find that funny, but Mort continued to chide me. His eyes widened as if a brilliant idea had flashed before him.

"I can see it now, your great advertising campaign—one of your Lakota Indians chasing a buffalo with a baseball bat."

"Baseball teams don't always need a product to endorse. Duke and I simply love the sport. Isn't that a good enough reason to own a team?"

"Perhaps, but I'm curious to know who hoodwinked you into paying for these Indians? I'm sure he's laughing all the way to the bank." Mort gave me a soft poke in the side.

"For your information, there was no middleman. I found this team. But I'll admit I took a great risk. It's good to take a risk now and then."

"Speaking of risk, how's Paul working out for you? He's very young."

"He may be young, but he has a good mind—couldn't be more proud of him. He's well liked, and because of his slaughterhouse experience, he knows the business from the ground up. I'm so confident in Paul that I could completely turn the operation over to him today and sleep well every night. That risk has so far paid great dividends."

"I suppose you're right about risk. You're always right," Mort said, standing up and removing his hat. "But not all risk taking is good. I should listen to you more often and the devil in me much less. My life is unraveling before my eyes. Jeanne found out about Ginny."

"What!" I said, standing up as well. I was shocked by the news, and Mort knew it.

"Shh…" Mort prompted. "Take your hat off."

We were both silenced by the National Anthem. And as I stood still looking at the flag and listening to the music, I knew that my friend's life was about to change drastically. Mort was on a sinking ship, and I couldn't help him. His job, his marriage, his status in the community, all could be in jeopardy.

We sat down after the music, and as Duke predicted, the umpires requested a time out—a ten minute delay. Duke was called out of the dugout and onto the field without any further explanation to the fans in the stadium.

While we waited for the game to begin, Mort poured out his soul to me.

"You were right about my Virginia. Guess I won't be calling her *my Ginny* any longer. It's bad, very bad. Yesterday she and Jeanne met face to face at the rental house, with me standing there in the room."

"That scene couldn't have been very civil."

"No, actually Jeanne was quite the lady in front of Ginny, and she was very civil around me, even after we arrived home. I know Jeanne was terribly hurt and upset, but she didn't want to show her pain."

"Of course she was hurt! How on earth did all of this happen?"

For once, I noticed that Mort felt some measure of disgrace, which gave me hope that his character was not as base as I had believed. Rather than look me straight in the eye, he explained the details as he looked down at his feet in shame.

"Yesterday morning I told Jeanne I would go to the ball park and watch my men practice. I missed a call at the house from my accountant. He left a short message with Jeanne, expressing his concern about the elderly widow who was renting the Hollywood house. He said that her rent was a week late, and it was odd because it usually came in the mail a little early. He suggested to Jeanne that I stop by to make sure the elderly woman was okay."

The concessioner, making his usual rounds, interrupted and asked, "Roasted peanuts?"

"Yes," I replied, reaching in my pocket for some loose change. "I'll take two bags. And keep the change."

"Thank you, sir."

I waited for him to be out of earshot before continuing my conversation. "Mort! How could that have happened when you were giving Ginny the rent money?"

"Ginny wasn't getting any studio parts, and she didn't tell me. She used it to pay for other living expenses. I could have found her some secretarial work at the radio station."

"I would think so. Your soap company certainly sponsors enough commercial time to influence a few producers."

"Jeanne knew I wouldn't be home for supper, so she decided to stop by the rental after some afternoon shopping. It's so unlike her to meddle in my business affairs, but so much like Jeanne to care about some elderly widow."

"Maybe Jeanne was a little suspicious, and your accountant's call gave her an opportunity to calm her worst fears."

"Yeah, I can see that now, but in this case, it validated them. I drove up to Hollywood and picked up Ginny. We went out for lunch, and afterwards, we went back to the rental for a few relaxing moments."

"I suppose without clothes."

"And that's when Jeanne knocked on the door. She wouldn't leave. She knocked a few times more and sat on one of the porch chairs, waiting for someone to answer. It was obvious that I was inside. My Duisenberg was parked in front of the house."

"And, of course, no one in that section of Hollywood owns a car like yours."

"I was trapped. At least when I opened the front door I was fully dressed."

Mort was so uncomfortable telling me this story that his voice cracked, but our wives were so close that he felt obligated to come clean with me.

"Here," I said, handing him a bag of peanuts. At this moment I knew Mort would have preferred a shot of gin, but he gratefully took the nuts.

"Thanks."

"And Ginny?" I asked.

"Ginny was still in the bedroom tidying the bed, but her hair was tussled and her lipstick smeared when she walked into the living room. Apparently I was wearing some of the red stuff as well. My shirt wasn't completely tucked in. It was awkward. Jeanne immediately introduced herself as Mrs. Morton Cunningham. She didn't ask for an explanation, and her silence was absolute torture. Jeanne and I left immediately after that. Thank goodness in separate cars. It made the ride home safe."

I listened to my friend. If there was any way I could help him, I would. "That's odd," I said. "Maggie didn't tell me about this run in, and surely Jeanne would have mentioned it to her."

"Maggie will know all about it before this game is over. The ladies are spending the afternoon together."

Since we were kids, Mort lived on the edge, admitting nothing to those he had hurt unless he was caught. His affair with Ginny was the most damaging thing he had ever done. He took a deep breath and exhaled. Mort was a prideful man, and it was not easy for him to admit guilt.

"I don't know what to tell you, Mort. We've all taken a few left turns in life, and then we seem to get back on course."

"But this time I turned left and drove over a cliff."

"You're not thinking of divorce—are you?"

"I can't get divorced. It will ruin me. What's worse, Jeanne knows if Father finds out about this, he'll remove me as president, and if he doesn't, the board of directors will."

"Their reaction would be that strong?"

"You know Father. He's been a church elder for years, and many of the board members have wanted to oust me over this factory expansion. I suspect they already have a replacement president in mind. Phin, there's nothing more important to me than my soap company. I could lose Jeanne, but not Silver Suds Soap."

Mort opened his bag of peanuts and shelled a few. Getting caught had paralyzed what little moral judgment was left in him. I had never known him to be fearful of anything, and yet my friend displayed all the signs of a scared rat.

"Life is inherently competitive," I told Mort. "We're all in a race against time, eventually leaving behind friends and unfulfilled desires, but the life-path we choose to race upon defines our character."

"In that regard, you and I are not alike."

"I suppose not. It would devastate me to lose Maggie, and I would forfeit everything I own to keep her. Life without her would be unimaginable. I want her there by my side when I rise in the morning and when I retire at night. Apart, I'm nothing. It saddens me, Mort, that you don't have the same attitude toward Jeanne. You don't know what you're missing."

"Maybe I don't. Jeanne will hold this—"

"Hold this affair over you? Mort, think about what you're saying. That's not the Jeanne I know. Have a serious talk with her. Own your mistake. Admit your guilt. But most importantly, change your ways and do whatever you must to repair your marriage."

Mort's eyes welled up. I knew he was taking my advice to heart, and I was glad, though mostly for Jeanne's sake.

"With your job hanging in the balance, Jeanne is the friend you need the most. Don't push her away."

"But what about Ginny?" Mort asked.

"Get that Hollywood starlet out of your rental house and out of your life at once! And I would postpone the start of your factory expansion to keep some of those board members happy. Has the land acquisition gone through?"

"Not yet, but we should be closing the deal soon."

"Change your offer." I paused for a moment to consider a few options. "Ask for a twelve month delay. Why must your factory startup date be October 1929? What's wrong with a construction groundbreaking in 1930 and a factory opening later that year? If your expansion is worthy, a short postponement won't matter. The election of Herbert Hoover this week should mean that our nation will be strong for the next several years. "

I continued to nibble on my peanuts. My friend was certainly in a bind, and yet I felt certain there was a solution.

"You think I could buy more time?" Mort asked.

"Yes, make the board feel like you're listening to them. A few hundred dollars may be all it takes to satisfy the seller of that land. It will cost you a little extra, but it may appease your shareholders by appearing more cautionary."

"Yes, I can see this working. A delay could mean higher dividends for the shareholders this quarter and perhaps next year. It could possibly salvage my job."

"More than salvaging your job, use the postponement to save your marriage. Spend a few months with Jeanne at your place on Catalina—just the two of you."

An announcement came over the public address system, "The situation on the field has been resolved and the game will commence."

The crowd broke out in loud cheers and whistles, interrupting my conversation momentarily.

"When Maggie traveled with me to South Dakota, they were some of our most pleasurable days. There were no distractions while we were on the train. It was just Maggie and me, the way I had always dreamed it would be. And because Paul has been running Gannon for several weeks with a great measure of success, I've had more lovely moments with my wife. I wish I could have more."

I placed my hand on his shoulder. "At least your problems have solutions. My problems are not that simple."

"Oh?"

"I'm dying, Mort. I won't be around much longer."

My friend briefly buried his face in his hands. He wanted to show concern, but as much as I liked Mort, I knew his inner reaction was all about his loss and not mine.

"It's your heart. Just like your father."

"I'm afraid it is."

"And the pills I saw you take in the bunkhouse—"

"They're for pain. There's no cure for a bad heart. So, I ask that you make me one final promise."

"Yes, of course."

"I want you to tough it out with Jeanne. Be faithful to her from this day forward. Be patient and hold onto her with all the tenderness you can muster. She deserves a husband who loves and respects her. Do it, Mort. Do it for you, for Jeanne, and for your sons. Do it because you are honor bound, and in doing so, you'll be doing it for me, even long after I'm gone."

~ Chapter Twenty-Eight ~

Mort and I could always depend on a good competition to provide us temporary relief from any sorrow or setback. It was like a healing balm, soothing our spirits in the middle of turmoil. And with his marital woes and my health issues, we were ready to enjoy the ballgame.

The center field flag pointed stiffly toward right as the stadium winds swirled in that direction. However, most of my attention was on the pitcher as the game began. Eagle Eye went into his wind-up and pitched the first ball. Pee-Wee Coultrain, the Suds' leadoff batter, was a short man who had the marvelous ability not just to hit the ball but to place it. He swung and connected near the end of his bat. The ball rocketed high into the air, drifting toward the right field line. It looked as though it would fall somewhere near Amos, a true testament to Pee-Wee's skill as a batter.

Amos could neither hear the crack of the bat, nor could he see the flight of the ball. He simply stood still without anticipation, as if he were selling cigars outside a tobacco shop.

"Foul!" The umpire shouted as the ball bounded into the stands to the great relief of Duke and me.

I saw Duke's foot tapping nervously as he sat on the dugout bench. He crossed his legs then uncrossed them again. The game was painful for us to watch when our weakest part of the outfield was on full display, beckoning batters to hit in Amos's direction. But Eagle Eye held his ground, impressing everyone with his pitching form and strength.

Maybe he could even strike Pee-Wee out, I thought as the count became full.

I saw Duke looking down at his feet. He could not stand to witness the tense moment as Eagle Eye threw the next pitch. I couldn't look down with Mort sitting next to me. It would have been too embarrassing.

Crack!

The sound forced Duke to look up and observe the ball. Again, it was a high rising ball that floated upward toward the heavens, heading for Amos in right field.

At this point no one could tell whether it would be fair or foul. The lingering high ball was too close to call.

"Please be foul. Please be foul," I cried.

Then something remarkable happened. Johnny Chasing Hawk sprinted out of center and across right field at an incredible pace. Watching his legs and feet move with such remarkable speed was an awesome sight. I knew that it would be nearly impossible for him to reach the ball in time, but he didn't despair because it looked like it would also be a foul ball. Another player, second baseman Fighting Bear, also saw the opportunity and immediately ran to the outfield in the direction of the ball. He turned around toward the infield, shielded his eyes from the sun with his glove, and regained sight of the ball. He waved off Chasing Hawk, and then hesitated as if he questioned the correctness of his call. The ball's downward velocity was sinking faster than he had expected. Fighting Bear suddenly realized that he could be short of the play. He picked up his pace toward the stands and dove for the ball. His extended body hit the ground and skidded across the rough grass until his left hand stretched across the foul line.

"Out!" The umpire shouted as the ball fell comfortably into Fighting Bear's glove.

Duke jumped to his feet, climbed up onto the roof of the dugout, and yelled over to Mort and me, "Eee-ha! Now that's what I call a ballplayer!"

My broad grin was so large it could be seen from all corners of the ballpark. I stood up and yelled back to Duke. "And he ran like that with boots on!"

I loved the look of shock on Mort's face as I sat down again.

"Humph," he grumbled. "Luck, that's all that play was."

"Luck? Ha! Did you see what my guy had to do to catch that ball? That wasn't luck. That was raw talent—raw Indian talent."

"We shall see. There are two more outs to go in this inning."

It was true. We had two more outs to go in the first, and the pressure was mounting. The fact that Pee-Wee was able to connect with David Eagle Eye's pitch and also direct his ball toward Amos only increased to my anxiety.

"Come on Eagle Eye!" I shouted. I held my breath while the next couple of pitches crossed the plate for batter number two. Both were balls, which added to the pressure of the moment.

Crack!

I could hear the ball and the bat connect. Again, the batter aimed for the weakest part of the outfield. But ah...so sweet—a line drive directly into the glove of our first baseman, Gordon Winter Cloud.

Two outs.

What a long and torturous inning, and there were eight more to go. Mort was right. The first two outs were beginner's luck for my amateur team who were about to be slaughtered by real ballplayers. I knew it, Duke knew it, and unfortunately Mort knew it.

The next batter was Mort's most expensive player and his best batter. I pretended to watch the game, but instead I focused my attention on Amos. How ridiculous it looked having a player stand in right field and not participate in the game, and how ridiculous of me to hire nine untested players from an Indian reservation—all because of an article I read in my doctor's office.

"Strike three!" the home plate umpire yelled.

Gracious! Did I miss something?

"Ha! Eagle Eye just struck out your best guy!" I stood up and hollered. "My Indian just took out your most expensive man!"

"Yeah, yeah, I saw it. He groused with a sour face.

Realizing that it would take too much time to get Amos off the field, Johnny Chasing Hawk ran over to Amos, bent down, and allowed the old man to grab on so he could carry him piggyback all the way to the dugout.

"Okay, men," Duke said as he clapped his hands a few times. "You kept the Suds from getting a hit, so all we need to do now is score."

Tom Fighting Bear was warming up his swing while the pitcher took his usual practice pitches. And then it was our time at bat.

Although the first pitch was a strike, it was a slight tip that caused the ball to hit the backstop. Fighting Bear's powerful swing made it obvious why he was our leadoff man.

Crack! A base hit into center field.

"We did it!" I yelled.

"You did nothing," Mort replied smugly. "It's only a base hit."

"But, Mort, don't you see the wonder in all of this? My guys have never before faced top professionals, and now we have a man on first."

"Calm down. Listening to you, one would think the Lakotas just won the game. It was just a base hit."

"That's what you think."

Duke put left fielder Luke Buffalo Warrior in the third base coach's box and ran over to first. He didn't expect the Lakota hit. In fact he was as dumfounded as I was. But now with a man on first, Duke was fully immersed in the game and excited to coach.

Running Deer was up to bat. I looked over at Duke. He was shifting his weight from side to side while punching his palm.

The Suds pitcher went into his wind-up and pitch.

Crack!

It was a bounding ball that the second baseman easily recovered without straying too far. He stepped on his bag and threw to first for an easy double play.

Bill Singing Wolf was now up to bat.

"Come on Singing Wolf," I yelled.

He was a big and imposing man. I thought for sure he could belt the ball over the fence.

The first pitch was a strike. It caught him looking.

"That's it, Singing Wolf. Hit the one you want," I yelled again.

The second pitch was a ball—low and outside.

And then the third pitch came.

Crack!

It was a high soaring ball heading deep into left field. I held my breath. It looked like it would clear the fence. But it was a little short, and the left fielder was right there to catch it.

My first three men were called out, but they all made contact with the ball. That was more than Morton's team could do in the first. Never before did I feel that being scoreless in baseball was as good as a win, but surviving tough opposition like the Silver Suds seemed unusually satisfying.

~ Chapter Twenty-Nine ~

Eagle Eye gave up two runs in the second. But by the third inning, our Lakotas charged back. Matthew Running Bull was in scoring position. With no outs, it was pitcher Eagle Eye's turn to bat. Amos would follow.

Of all times to have Amos up to bat, I thought. We finally got a man on base, and it was about to be his turn.

Duke had left his place in the first base coach's box and headed for the dugout just before it was time for Amos's warm-up.

"Okay, Amos," Duke said, helping him up off the bench. "You're gonna get a chance at the plate. Do nothing but stand still, and you'll be fine."

"I can do that."

"Good, because it's important."

Duke escorted Amos out of the dugout.

"See that circle on the ground?"

"Yes."

"You need to stand in the middle of that circle until it's your turn. Can you see the umpire? He's the big fellow over there in dark clothing."

Amos stared in that direction. "I see him."

"The catcher squats down in front of the umpire, and the plate is in front of the catcher.

"I remember."

"Good. Do you remember the rules about the batter's box?"

"Yes, I must stand in the batter's box."

"Either side of the plate is fine. For you—it won't matter. Their pitcher will throw three times down the middle and over the plate for an easy out. Okay, Amos, I have to go back to my spot by first base. Remember, don't swing, just stand and wait until the umpire calls you out. As soon as he declares strike three, return to the dugout."

"How will I know when it's my turn to bat?"

"Listen for your name. The announcer will say *Amos Wise Heart* when it's your time to bat. If you're not sure, listen for your teammates. They'll let you know. They'll help you out. You'll do fine."

Amos's name was announced after David Eagle Eye was called out on strikes. Running Bull remained on second. With one out and a little coaxing from everyone, including the umpire and the Suds' catcher, Amos shuffled over to the batter's box. Though his hands were incorrectly placed on the bat, he managed to take his stance.

"Hey, you old Indian," a spectator yelled. "This is a young man's sport. Get off the field and go back to your reservation."

His unkind remarks encouraged a few more rude spectators to join in the name calling. Amos didn't react. He stood at the plate with great aplomb as the first two pitches were called strikes.

"Look at that—the old man can't swing!" Mort's third baseman yelled. This also provoked more spectators to laugh.

Duke, standing in the coach's box at first, looked directly into the first baseman's eyes. "So help me, if you say anything derogatory to that old Indian, I'll see to it that you never play California winter ball again."

Amos kept his dignity in the face of such humiliation, but in direct defiance to Duke's instructions, he decided to swing the bat—a practice swing one might call it, though Amos's poor eyesight kept him from knowing the difference. He swung, much like a child trying to hit a piñata. The twisting motion of his body caused him to lose his balance and fall to the ground.

The umpire, wanting to keep the game moving along, called it *strike three* and the second out of the inning. He helped Amos to his feet with a little assistance from the catcher.

Many spectators sitting near Mort and me laughed, and Mort joined in.

"This is too much," Mort said as he doubled up. He could hardly contain himself as he slapped my shoulder. "I've never had so much fun watching a game."

Here was my friend whom I had known nearly all my life. He cheated on his wife and laughed at an elderly man who was only trying to save his team by being a symbolic placeholder. I wanted to call Mort a jackass—but I didn't.

"It takes courage to face adversity with dignity," I said. "You could learn a few things about tact, humility, and especially respect from that old guy."

"I probably could." Mort continued to laugh so hard he began to wheeze. "But I won't learn a thing about baseball."

Amos walked away from the plate with his head held high, but unfortunately he was walking toward the wrong dugout. In the excitement of his fall, Amos had become disoriented, and his poor eyesight confused him more.

Duke ran to Amos's side, placing his arm around him.

"It's this way, Amos. You're a little turned around. Our dugout is over here."

Amos finally made his way back to the correct side where he was consoled by his fellow tribesmen.

"It's okay," Bill Singing Wolf said. "We only have two outs and another chance to score in this inning."

Second baseman Tom Fighting Bear took his place in the batter's box. It was the top of the Lakota order. As the taunting continued, it fueled Fighting Bear's resolve to get a hit.

"Hey, you red-faced old dog, you play ball like a woman," a spectator hollered. Again, several others seated around the stadium joined in.

Fighting Bear clenched his teeth. This was a new experience for the Lakotas, who were only acquainted with gentlemanly games on the reservation and at the Carlisle School. He tightened his grip. He was up for a fight, a fight for the game and a fight for honor.

Back in the dugout, Singing Wolf was furious. He told Amos how much he resented the way the crowds and the other team treated their elder and the other players, but Amos remained calm.

"Amos," Singing Wolf spoke angrily, "this California country is not for Lakota, and we should leave at once."

"No, my son," Amos replied. "This is all about our team and our people. We are here. As a team we have already tasted our victory and should never concede it to the other team. We should stay and demonstrate victory with honor."

"Then tying the score this inning would be sweet justice." Singing Wolf slapped his hand against the dugout wall and turned his frustration around by singing out to Fighting Bear in soothing melodic native tones.

"That is good, Singing Wolf," Amos said. "You must continue to stand tall for our team and for all Lakota people."

Fighting Bear heard the soulful chant and reacted with a nod.

Hank Hudson, the Suds' seasoned pitcher, was no stranger to tough situations. He had pitched for Boston before moving on to Philadelphia and Cleveland. The Lakotas appeared to be no threat to his experienced arm. He went into his wind-up and release, but Fighting Bear's determination reached beyond the pitcher's abilities. He swung and connected with the ball. It was a sound very familiar to professionals, a solid hit. The ball rocketed high into the air.

Duke closely followed the ball, as did Mort and I.

Please, please, please, I said under my breath, begging the ball to clear the left field fence.

And then, it did!

"He did it it! He did it!" I stood up and shouted.

Duke jumped up and down as I roared with great joy. We had been suddenly cleansed of all doubt regarding our players. They were truly ready for this game. After Fighting Bear's powerful home run, we realized that our Lakotas had an honest chance for a Los Angeles slot.

"Come," Singing Wolf said to Amos as he grabbed his arm. "We should congratulate Fighting Bear as he rounds third base."

Amos agreed.

So with the help of Singing Wolf, Amos made it out to the third base line to cheer on their fellow player.

I continued to stand and applaud. I was so proud of these young men who, win or lose, were going to give the Suds a real fight.

The tone of the crowd seemed to shift. They were now amazed by our Lakota players and showed their appreciation for such remarkable talent by cheering for Fighting Bear as he rounded the bases and headed for home plate.

With the score tied, it was Running Deer's turn at bat. I could feel the tension mounting as the count became full.

Sadly, *strike three* was the final call. But as the game entered the top of the fourth, I felt, for the first time since I hired my Lakotas, that I was getting my money's worth.

~ CHAPTER THIRTY ~

As the game wore on, there were a few hits on both sides, but the score remained tied at two apiece. Both pitchers were impressive, and my fielders Chasing Hawk and Buffalo Warrior continued to wow the crowds by covering the vast outfield. With no break in the score, I was beginning to wonder if the game would go long.

Once again, it was Amos's time to bat. The umpire seemed to be a mellow sort of gentleman who grew increasingly patient with the elderly Sioux each time he slowly shuffled his feet all the way to the batter's box. Amos had since learned how to hold the bat, but this time his body was in harm's way.

The pitcher looked at Amos and saw how he crowded the plate. There was very little room to pitch the ball over the plate without hitting him.

The catcher turned to the umpire. "Can you tell a batter that he's going to get hurt if he stands like that?"

"You just did, but I don't think he understands."

"Well, he's a grown man, ump."

"He is that. Come on," the umpire said. "Let's keep this game moving."

"I hope you're ready," the catcher said with great doubt.

"I'm fine," Amos replied calmly and proudly.

"Okay, have it your way." The catcher crouched into position.

The Suds' pitcher was amused. He felt talented enough to avoid hitting Amos, but should Amos lean forward or shift his weight at the wrong moment, he could possibly take a terrible blow.

Duke, standing in the first base coach's box, could see the possibility of Amos winding up on first base. This was the last thing Duke wanted because the old Indian had no idea what to do as a runner.

The first two pitches were easy strikes, but the third pitch was disastrous, grazing Amos on his forearm. Amos clenched his teeth and held his arm close to his chest until the pain subsided.

"Are you okay?" the umpire asked.

"Yes, I'll be fine. It's not as bad as a snakebite."

"Whatever you say, Mr. Indian." The umpire waved off Duke, indicating that Amos was fine, just as Amos started to shuffle toward the dugout.

"Hey, old fellow, come back here. This time you're taking a base. There's no going back to the bench."

"Amos!" Duke yelled. "This way. Walk toward me."

Amos took four and then five steps toward first base.

"That's it, Amos," Duke continued to yell. "Walk this way toward this white bag!"

Amos was bewildered, but he soon realized that this situation was a little different and continued to trek toward first using his bat as a cane.

"You're doing fine, Amos," Duke continued to yell. "Keep coming this way, until you reach first base. That's it! Now put the bat down, Amos. Just toss it off to your side, and keep coming. Amos, you have to put the bat down!"

Amos finally dropped his bat as he neared first.

Mort began laughing uncontrollably, which only agitated me until my chest began to tighten. I could feel tiny beads of sweat gathering above my upper lip, so I reached into my breast pocket for my handkerchief and pill vial.

"Oh, Phin." Mort continued to laugh. "I can see why you need to take a pill now! You'll soon have to get out your checkbook, too. That old Indian of yours is going to give this game to my Suds."

"Nonsense!" I replied just before I swallowed my medicine. "This game isn't over, and if you ask me, our Lakotas are doing just fine. I fully believe that once our third baseman recovers from his injuries, we'll be contenders for the playoffs! You'll see!"

Within a minute I was feeling much better. I thought I had returned my pill vial to my breast pocket, but it didn't make it. I was so involved in the game that I didn't notice the small bottle had bypassed my jacket, fell by my feet, and rolled under the stadium seat.

By this time I could tell that Duke was deeply concerned with the current situation. How was he going to get Amos to second base and beyond without incident?

"Amos." Duke pointed to second base. "Can you see that white bag over there?"

Amos squinted and then pointed as well. "Yes, I think so?"

"That's your next base, and as soon as I yell *run*, start heading for that bag. Should you make it to that bag, listen for Chasing Hawk's voice. He's standing in the third base coach's box. He will tell you what to do."

Amos nodded.

I was positive about only one thing. Duke's instructions to Amos were meaningless.

It was the top of the Lakota order, and Fighting Bear was once again up to bat. If only he could hit another home run, I thought, then coaching Amos to home plate would be the next big challenge, though certainly not impossible.

The pitcher went into his wind-up, then his release. Fighting Bear swung hard, and Duke instantly felt it was at least a double. "Run, Amos. Run!" Duke shouted.

Amos began to waddle toward second base. To Duke's great surprise, the Suds' center fielder, a seasoned semipro from Vernon— one of Los Angeles County's best local teams—made an incredible catch. Amos, who was still shuffling down the baseline toward second, was doomed. It was an easy double play for the Suds. The inning was over, and the score remained tied.

~ CHAPTER THIRTY-ONE ~

"Would you like to double that bet of ours?" Mort joked.

It was now the bottom of the ninth inning. The Lakotas were down by one run with a man on first base. I could not see a way for my team to win, knowing that my pitcher, whose batting average was under .200, was up next. And he would be followed at the plate by Amos.

"No, Mort, I don't wish to accept your sucker bet."

A great feeling of disappointment fell upon me as I thought about all the time and money spent hiring this team, not to mention the expenses I incurred in order to have the Lakotas entered into the Los Angeles winter ball trial. It was a business gamble, and at this point all I could see were financial losses for my efforts. Without a win today, there was no hope of recouping the bulk of my losses. It was at this moment that I decided, win or lose, my Lakotas could stay in California until the winter ball season was over. Most of the necessary money had already been spent. Finding an inland league wouldn't cost me that much more, and it would help their impoverished village. They had family and expenses, and it would be better to dig deeper into my pockets and subsidize them than to send them back with only a mere stipend for playing one game.

My attention turned to Duke, and I noticed him in a face to face discussion with Amos. It looked too serious to ignore. I knew it was almost his turn at bat, and it appeared as if Amos had some serious reservations about nearing the plate after being struck by a pitch. This would automatically throw the game to the Silver Suds.

I walked toward the Lakota dugout, getting as close as I could. "Duke," I called out.

His head popped up when he heard my voice. "Amos wants to throw the game," Duke said to me. "He doesn't want to bat."

Amos looked up as well.

"Amos, may I ask a favor of you?" I said. "All I want you to do is listen. I know that you're frightened of the baseball because you can't see it whizzing by, so this can't be easy for you. But even though you may have poor eyesight, God has blessed you with good insight. You once told me that you walk by faith and not by sight. I know that it takes all kinds of gifts to make a great Indian nation, and it takes all sorts of talents to make this great Lakota ball club. You, Amos, understand this concept well. You have kept this team pure Lakota, so your teammates can boldly return to South Dakota and say that you fought the good fight as one people. The umpire will soon call you to the plate. Your team needs you to bat just this last time. You're one of the great elders of your tribe. Today you must find and demonstrate your inner strength for your teammates. Come, Amos, grab your bat. Eagle Eye has been called to the plate."

As I returned to my seat, Duke helped Amos to the on deck circle.

I looked down upon the field and saw Amos raise his bat above his head. He began to sing a prayer similar to the one I had heard Friday night at the ranch. When his song was over, he took a couple of practice swings.

"Hey, I don't believe it," Mort said. "Your old guy wants to swing this time."

"Nah, it's just a ritual. He can't see, so why would he swing?"

"That's exactly what I was thinking."

The count for Eagle Eye was full. Though not consistent, Eagle Eye would, on occasion, connect and surprise the crowds. The Silver Suds pitcher went into his wind-up and pitch.

Eagle Eye swung.

Crack!

The bat made the wonderful sound of a solid hit. To the crowd, it looked like a stand-up double. The play was at home, and knowing this, Eagle Eye took a bold risk and stretched his hit into a triple.

"Safe!" the home plate umpire yelled with his arms stretched wide as the runner from first base crossed home plate with a dusty slide.

The score was now tied, and Eagle Eye was on third. I was somewhat relieved, knowing that Amos's failure at the plate would only mean two outs with one man on third and the top of the order to follow. At the very least, the game could go into extra innings.

The Silver Suds' pitcher was now confident and a bit cocky. What pitcher wouldn't be? Amos was nearly blind, could barely walk, and had the swing of a nine-year-old.

"As long as my pitcher doesn't hit the old guy with a pitch, this will be an easy out," Mort said.

Like every other time when it was Amos's time at bat, his general appearance and mannerisms had a relaxing effect on the Silver Suds, both in the infield and the outfield. Even the Suds' pitcher Hank Hudson let down his guard as everyone patiently watched the elderly tribesman shuffle his feet all the way to the batter's box, using his bat like a cane for stability.

Amos took his place, and to the amazement of all those present, he stood on the left-hander's side of home plate.

"Hey, it looks like you got a switch hitter there," Mort chided me. His laugh was absolutely annoying.

"Can I close my eyes?" Amos asked the umpire.

The catcher laughed out loud. "Hey, ump, there's nothing in the rule book that says a batter has to have his eyes open, is there?"

"Yeah, you can close 'em. It probably won't matter," the umpire replied, shaking his head. Never before had he witnessed a batter so afraid of the ball that he wanted to close his eyes. "Sure, you can close 'em, if you like."

The catcher chuckled while signaling to the pitcher what to throw.

Amos clenched his eyes shut, deepening the wrinkles all over his face and temples.

The umpire, catcher, and pitcher held back laughter, but not their pompous grins.

The pitcher went into his first wind-up and pitch. Amos took a surprising swung, something Duke had warned him not to do. But the bat miraculously connected, and the ball soared gently into the air, inches above the first baseman's reach. The right fielder, also standing flat-footed and without regard, was slow to react. What he had presumed impossible had just happened.

Duke was dumbfounded. He could barely believe it—an old blind man would drive in the winning run.

"Hurry, Amos!" Duke yelled. "This way! You gotta come this way."

Amos began his slow trek down the first base line.

"Put the bat down!" Duke frantically waved his arms, hoping Amos would comply.

"Where?"

"Anyplace!"

Amos dropped his bat and was barely halfway toward first base when the right fielder recovered the ball and threw it toward home plate.

Although the Suds' catcher was in position when the ball rocketed into his mitt from right field, Eagle Eye's foot had already tagged home plate.

"Safe!" the umpire yelled. Even he had a look of disbelief.

The crowd went wild, cheering and chanting like Indians. The Lakotas won the game with Amos's unbelievable connection of bat with ball.

Duke could barely contain himself. He grabbed Amos, lifted him up, and carried him back toward the dugout. "Do you know what you just did? You just won the game! You just made my wildest dream come true!"

The Lakota players poured out of the dugout onto the field singing a native chant.

Mort's face had a ghostly appearance. He couldn't believe his eyes, and neither could all the other fans in the stands.

"Oh, Mort, I'm so sorry." I began to laugh. In fact, I was laughing so hard my sides began to ache.

"Sure you're sorry. I can see it all over you."

Mort's cranky reply humored me even more.

"Phineas, the only thing you're sorry about is that you didn't take me up on my sucker bet." He handed me five, one hundred dollar bills.

I continued to laugh. "What a hit that was! Who would have ever believed Amos would win the game? Excuse me, Mort, but I've got to get down onto the field and congratulate my men."

With each step I took toward the field, I thought about my entire Lakota adventure. If it hadn't been for my first heart attack when Mort and I raced our Miller cars, I might have never seen the article in *Holbrook's Magazine.* And although it would be my last competition with Mort, this baseball game represented all of the loose ends in my life. I could completely retire now that Paul had taken over Gannon Fine Meats. Maggie and I could set sail for Europe, and my new friend Amos and the rest of his Oglala tribe could have an income, not just for this year, but with all the positive publicity about to surround my team, surely they could benefit a few more years to come.

Duke approached me as I walked onto the field.

"We did it!" Duke said, shaking my hand. "We jumped over the moon! Our Lakotas just beat Mort's pros!"

"I'm still having difficulty believing it myself, and can you imagine how the *Times* and the *Herald* are going to report this? What a game! I can't wait to see the morning papers."

"I know what they're going to say," Travis Maxwell said, as he approached us. The press box is all abuzz with excitement. Some are even calling it, *The Game of the Twentieth Century.* I can't wait to call my publisher with this story. Your Los Angeles Lakotas will be a national sensation before month's end!"

I continued to congratulate my players, and then I saw Amos. I took his hand and filled it with the money I had just won. "Here's five hundred dollars. It's your winnings for today's game and money your people could use."

"Thank you, my friend."

"You are most welcome, but who on earth told you when to swing that bat?"

"No one on earth, although Duke gave me the idea. He told me that the pitcher would always throw a blind man three pitches right down the middle and over the plate, so I knew all I had to do was swing."

"All you had to do was swing? You've got to be kidding!" I replied.

"I closed my eyes and concentrated on the sounds, and when the Great Spirit moved me, I swung."

I laughed and laughed, and I almost got Amos to laugh, as well. But then I felt a severe pain in my chest. I needed to sit down. I was having difficulty speaking. I began to sweat heavily. I reached into my breast pocket for my pill vial. It wasn't there. I panicked. I needed to sit down, but before I could reach the dugout bench, my knees buckled. I felt my body hit the ground. My face pressed against the dirt.

Duke, who was not far away, yelled, "Phin!" He dropped to my side. "Help!" he yelled. "I need some help over here! A doctor—we need a doctor!" Duke continued to yell as he ran for help.

Although my eyes were opened, I couldn't see, but I knew that Amos had knelt down by my side.

"Amos, what's going on here?" I asked.

"God has allowed you to see this important victory."

"And I did see it. Our team was sensational. You were sensational."

"No, Phineas. It was the Great Spirit of God. He was sensational."

I suddenly felt much better, so I stood up, coming face to face with Mort. "After all these years of competition, I wound up a hundred dollars ahead." I laughed, but Mort wasn't laughing. He wasn't even looking at me. He was looking down at my feet.

I looked down, too, and saw my body lying in the dirt near the dugout. Mort got on his knees, lifting my head up slightly. I felt his hands around my head, while Amos held my hand.

"He's still alive!" Mort said just under his breath. He eased my head down, stood up, and yelled, "Where's that stadium doctor?"

What's going on here? How can this be? From above I could see Amos beside me. It was odd. I was looking down at Amos, yet I could feel him touching my shoulder as my body lay on the ground. I could also hear his soft words spoken in his native language. I was delirious and unsure of my whereabouts.

"Your pure Lakota team won the game," I said to Amos. "It was a great victory for you."

"Yes, Phin, we beat the white man, and you beat your friend Morton. And now, with our team in the winter ball league, we will earn enough money to keep our families comfortable this winter."

I was able to breathe much better as my eyes came into focus. There, directly above me was Amos—his weathered face a joy to see. "This is not the way I wanted to say goodbye."

"Phin," Amos replied. "There are no *goodbyes* in my language. You should learn to say *akewachinyakinkte*." He pronounced it *a-kay-wa-che-ya-kintay.* "It means I want to see you again."

It was true. I didn't want to say goodbye. I wanted to see my friend again, and I wanted to see my Maggie, too. Akewachinyakinkte, the strange word gave me a measure of hope.

"*Akewachinyakinkte*, Amos."

"That's much better, my friend. There will be more tomorrows for us. You'll see."